# THE RESCUED BRIDE'S SAVIOR

## BEAR CREEK BRIDES BOOK ONE

### AMELIA ROSE

# CONTENTS

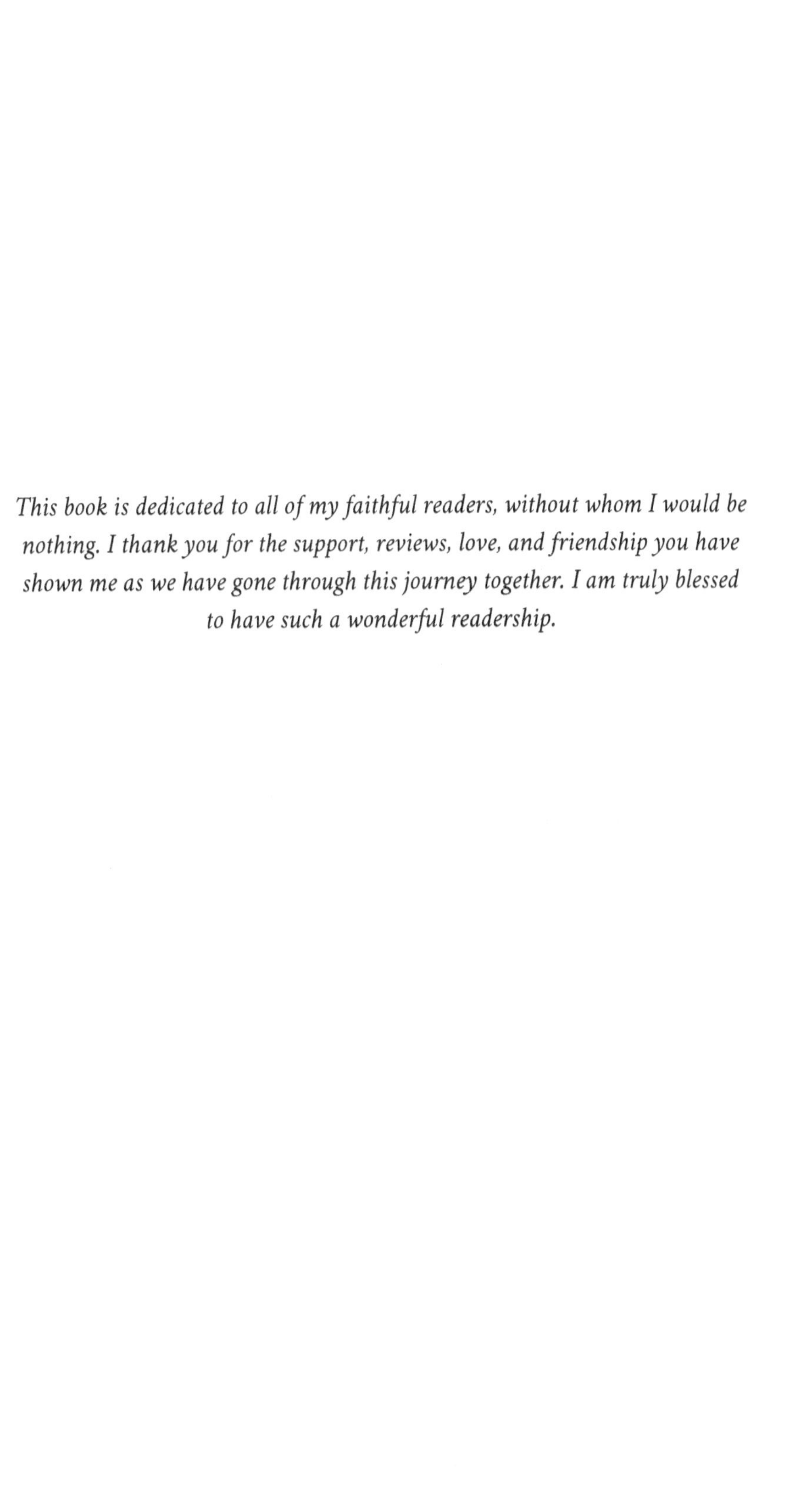

*This book is dedicated to all of my faithful readers, without whom I would be nothing. I thank you for the support, reviews, love, and friendship you have shown me as we have gone through this journey together. I am truly blessed to have such a wonderful readership.*

# PREFACE

Mrs. Phillips was at home with her daughter when it all happened. They were together in the sitting room, enjoying afternoon tea with close friends. An intricate but graceful Chinese floral wallpaper had been picked out for the lined and swagged curtains, accessorized with bronze fringing, providing a perfect setting for sofas and chairs with their yellow and dark blue chintz. Mrs. Phillips and her eighteen-year-old daughter Jenny were entertaining three of their dearest friends, a mother and two daughters. That afternoon, Mrs. Phillips had asked that the very best, dark blue and gold Crown Derby china from England was to be used and Cook had produced some sumptuous cakes. The air was full of gossip and laughter. Suddenly, Mr. Phillips came running through the front door and slammed it against the wall. The women in the sitting room jumped with fright and were overcome with astonishment. Then, when Mr. Phillips started yelling madly, Mrs. Phillips felt a shudder of fear run down her spine.

"Margret! Margret!" Mr. Phillips called for his wife. Mrs. Phillips stood slowly, gave her guests a kind smile and quickly left the sitting room. The moment she stepped into the hallway, Mr. Phillips was upon her. He gripped her shoulders roughly, his skin drained of color as he panted and found it hard to catch his breath.

"Margret, you must get Jenny and leave immediately. The constable and the deputies are on their way," Mr. Phillips said frantically.

"What on earth are you speaking of, Douglas? Why are you so frightened?" she asked her husband, a man she'd loved for many years.

"No time to explain now. It will no doubt be written in the papers by morning." He seemed to realize he'd been gripping his wife's shoulders too hard. He gently caressed them, his hands moving up and down her arms as he looked upon his wife for what would no doubt be the last time.

"Now, get Jenny and get out of here. Duke is already waiting for you outside in the carriage," Mr. Phillips said and pointed to the open door. "You can come back later for your things."

"Douglas, I don't like this. Why won't you tell me anything?" Mrs. Phillips pleaded with her husband, a terrible feeling of foreboding washing over her.

"All in time, my love," Mr. Phillips said in a terribly sad voice. "Now go." Mr. Phillips took one more look at his wife before moving past her and throwing open the sitting room doors. He headed straight toward his daughter, ignoring the other women present. This was not the time for civility. He needed to ensure that his wife and daughter were not present for what was about to happen.

"Come, Jenny. Your mother needs you," Mr. Phillips said as he helped his daughter to her feet. She looked concerned – her lovely auburn hair done up in curls that framed her puzzled face. Jenny's sky blue eyes shone brightly as ever, and Mr. Phillips hated the idea of making her cry. Due, though, to the consequences of his poor choices, her tears were unavoidable.

"But, Father. We have guests," Jenny said as she was led out of the room by her father, her pale-yellow silk gown swishing around her as she went. She looked over her shoulder at her friends as they stared, watching helplessly as she left the room in a hurry.

"Jenny, go with your mother now. Uncle Duke is in the carriage waiting for you," Mr. Phillips instructed as he let go of her hand. Jenny looked to her mother, who looked as confused as she felt. She saw a look pass between her parents before her mother took her hand and led her quickly from the house.

Jenny wanted to ask her father why their afternoon tea party had been interrupted or why they should leave the house immediately. A feeling of fear and fright wound its way through her as she held her mother's hand tightly, she picked up her skirts and walked carefully down the front steps of their home in Richmond, Virginia. She still wore her house slippers as there had not been time to change into proper walking shoes.

As described, Uncle Duke sat in his phaeton carriage looking off in the distance. He appeared to be trying his best to ignore whatever was happening. As Jenny's mother led her by the hand, the driver hopped down from the front seat to help Mrs. Phillips into the back with her uncle and then to help Jenny into the front with him.

"Duke, what is going on?" Margret demanded to know. Jenny looked over her shoulder at her uncle, but the man refused to make eye contact with either of them.

Then, as though Jenny thought she was fading into a dream, men ran up the stairs and swarmed her home. They wore official uniforms and had various badges on their chests. Shouts filled the air, followed by the sound of gunfire. Duke commanded his driver to take off as Jenny and Mrs. Phillips covered their mouths in horror, fearing the worst.

Jenny sobbed into her silk-gloved hand as her other held onto the side of the carriage. She strained her neck to see what was happening in her home. She heard women shouting and saw her friends run out of her home and down the steps. She wanted to ask them what had happened, but the carriage had pulled away from the house as the horses increased their pace.

Jenny wasn't sure what was happening, but whatever had happened to her father, she knew it wasn't good.

# CHAPTER 1

athew Jenkins sat on the front porch of his small ranch home. He rested in a rocking chair, one that his father had made for his mother when Mathew was born. The sturdy oak chair had held up all these years, and as Mathew watched the sun set, his cattle dog, Bailey, by his side, he thought the setting sun looked a little sad this evening.

Mathew ran his fingers through his dark brown hair. Soon he'd need a haircut, but sometimes he liked his hair to hang around his shoulders. When he was in town, he knew that the longer hair was unseemly. But when he was in camp with his Indian friends, he almost fit right in. But now as Mathew watched the sun with only the sound of chirping crickets breaking the silence, he suddenly felt very lonely and almost out of place.

The day had been long and the work hard. Yet, he was used to it. He'd been cattle ranching since the day he could ride a horse. His father had been a rancher when he first came to settle in Montana. Mathew knew how to watch over the herd, move them to the other fenced-in pasture when they needed fresh grass, and how to drive them to market. In fact, Mathew had recently returned from the auctions after selling some of his finest cattle. The journey usually took three weeks to complete as he drove his cattle to the auction site that resided on the outskirts of Idaho. Ranchers came from all over the territories to sell and buy cattle. Mathew always looked forward to his time at the auctions because it reminded him so much of his fond memories he had with his father doing the same thing.

Mathew was certain he'd be set for the winter since it was only him and Bailey at the ranch. Next week he'd start filling the cellar with supplies for the impending winter now only weeks away. Mathew still remembered the series of disastrous winters ten years ago when most of the ranchers in Montana lost over half of their herd. It was why his herd was so small compared to the ranchers he met at the markets in Idaho, but he'd learned to live on the small amount he had and to also prepare for each coming winter as though it would be the worst one yet.

But as he sighed deeply, knowing another good day's work was complete, he couldn't help but feel like his life was missing something. Absentmindedly, Mathew leaned forward in the rocker and petted Bailey, the collie raising his head and wagging his tail at the feel of Mathew's fingers running through his fur. Mathew smiled down at his trusty companion, trying to remind himself that he wasn't completely alone. Bailey had been given to him as a puppy when he turned eighteen, a sign of true responsibility, and as Mathew had trained the pup to be a good cattle dog, Mathew knew that Bailey would always be his best friend.

Living out in Bear Creek came with a lot of pros and cons. When Mathew had finished the eighth grade, he left school and started working full-time for his father. It was what most young boys did at his age, and he was proud to do so. But with working every day came many challenges. For one, Mathew then didn't make it into town that often to see his friends. Sometimes the different ranchers would do cattle drives together or help out during the harvest season to collect all the hay from the farmers. But as the years went on, Mathew saw less and less of his school friends. And now with both his parents having passed on, the ranch that had been his childhood home now only echoed of memories gone by.

He was so lost in his thoughts, so focused on the setting sun, that he didn't even hear Brown Bear come walking out of the shadows and settle onto the front steps of the porch. It was only when Bailey moved from his reach that Mathew looked down to see the smiling Indian looking up at him. Mathew scoffed at himself, knowing that at any minute the Indian chief would tease him for being unguarded.

"How's it going, Brown Bear?" Mathew asked when the older man remained silent.

"It is a chilly evening, Mathew. I came to visit, to see if you'd returned from the cattle market," Brown Bear said. Mathew noted the tone of his voice and the hint of sadness. He sighed, fearing he was about to hear of troubles the local Sioux Indians were facing. Ever since the battle at Wounded Knee two years ago when one hundred forty-five Sioux were gunned down by the Seventh Cavalry, Brown Bear and his people had remained quiet and to themselves in the mountains surrounding Bear Creek. Though a few came to town and were friendly with everyone, Mathew was continually concerned about the military one day coming to Bear Creek to push out the Sioux people, or worse, take all their lives without mercy.

"It's a bit chilly, Brown Bear. But nothing to be worried about. But I feel that the weather is not what concerns you."

Brown Bear smiled as he nodded, the raven feathers in his hair seeming to dance as he did so. He wore a deer-hide tunic and trousers, his feet were clothed in moccasins. Round his neck he wore the bone necklaces of a chieftain, beautifully constructed with beads and feathers. But all of the authority he held over his tribe seemed to fade as he simply sat on Mathew's front porch.

"The miners won't back off of our lands, Mathew. They are scaring away all the deer with their dynamite as they try to find gold and precious stones within the mountain," he said with a heavy heart. Mathew could see the frustration and annoyance in the Chief's eyes.

"Have you gone to speak to Sheriff Benning about it, Brown Bear?"

Mathew folded his arms and leaned back into the rocker. His mind started to think of the quickest, possible solution. Mathew may not have been the best at reading and writing at school, but problem solving was always his special talent.

"Tensions are rising, I have forbidden all interaction between camp and town. There is nothing my people can't gather for the impending winter from our lands. It was simply nice to trade with the locals while things were peaceful." Another deep sigh left the Chief, and Mathew could only assume that the decision had come with much heaviness. The Sioux Indians had always been very friendly with the locals in Bear Creek. But the more the miners tried to dig close to the Indian's camp, the more issues started to arise.

"That is understandable, Brown Bear. I truly wish you and your people all the best," Mathew said as his mind kept running through different action possibilities. "I will speak with Sheriff Benning this week when I go to town for supplies."

Brown Bear straightened his posture and grunted his approval. "Thank you, Mathew. It is much appreciated to have you as our ally." Mathew only nodded, thinking about the last time he helped the Sioux. He'd been in the hills hunting for local game when he found himself in a skirmish between the miners and Indians. It had been Mathew's diplomatic voice of reason that ended the fight without anyone sustaining injuries. He'd earned Brown Bear's respect then. But if the miners continued to push, there might not be anything anyone would be able to do when the Sioux rose up to defend themselves and their people.

"Don't thank me just yet, Brown Bear. Until the miners do something that Sheriff Benning can haul them off to jail for, we may not be able to do anything to solve the situation."

"We shall not talk of this issue any longer, Mathew. It is not the only reason I have come tonight," Brown Bear said, his authoritarian voice returning. Mathew smiled encouragingly, curious to know what Brown Bear might say next.

"I have a message from the Great Spirit to give to you." He stood, his eyes locking with Mathew's. Mathew looked into Brown Bear's obsidian depths and knew that an Indian Chief was speaking directly to him. "The Great Spirit wants you to know that the time has come for you to fill your home with more people. As winter approaches, you should claim yourself a wife."

Even though Brown Bear spoke with great sincerity, Mathew couldn't help but give a gut-wrenching laugh. He wrapped his arms around his body as he shook with mirth.

"Forgive me, Brown Bear," Mathew said between gasps for air. He didn't want to disrespect the Chief but couldn't believe his words. "I would have never guessed the Great Spirit would burden you with such a message."

"It is no burden at all, Mathew," Brown Bear said as he narrowed his eyes at his friend. "But it is no less very serious. The Great Spirit doesn't bless me with these messages just to be laughed at." Brown Bear wasn't hurt by Mathew's laughter, but he never passed up an opportunity to tease his friend.

"I don't doubt that, Brown Bear. I simply think it's humorous that the Great Spirit would want me to get married. I'm not Indian, after all." Mathew said as he ran his fingers through his hair. He found it odd that Brown Bear was speaking of the exact same thing he'd been thinking of earlier on in the evening.

"Yet, you are still a human just like me," Brown Bear said with a raised eyebrow as though to challenge Mathew to disagree with him.

"Yes, that is true," Mathew said with a sigh. "So, a wife by winter, huh?"

Brown Bear gave him a wide smile as he nodded firmly. "It will be good for you to have someone to keep you warm during the long winter months." He tried his best to keep down the chuckle that threatened to bubble up.

"Oh yeah? Is there a particular Indian maiden that you would recommend, Brown Bear?" Mathew said with a sly smile.

Brown Bear did chuckle then. He shook his head, knowing how teasing Mathew could be. He reminded him of his younger brother who was very similar in character. "You must marry one of your own, Mathew. There is already tension enough between the two people of this land," Brown Bear spoke honestly. "And I doubt you'd give up your ranch to live the Indian way."

Mathew nodded he knew that his friend spoke the truth. "You are right, Brown Bear. I would never give up this ranch, and I'm sure a maiden would never want to give up her way of life."

"Very wise, Mathew. Therefore, you must look for a wife elsewhere."

Mathew thought about the idea for a moment. He knew that the options in Bear Creek were very limited. Women were either elderly or married. As he wondered about where he could meet a potential wife, Mathew remembered the conversation he had with a ranch hand in Idaho. The man had talked about meeting his wife as a mail-order-bride. She'd come from Boston to Idaho, their meeting had been arranged. The two were now married, and happily so.

"Brown Bear, have you ever heard of a mail-order-bride before?" Mathew asked as he leaned forward and began to pet Bailey once more. He felt silly for even talking to an Indian about this idea.

"No, Mathew. What does this White term mean?" Brown Bear asked curiously.

"Well, the idea would be that I would post an ad in the newspapers in the East. I would advertise for a bride and interested ladies would then write to me in response to the ad. And after we've communicated through letters, she would eventually come here with the intent to marry." Mathew spoke slowly, trying to make sure that his friend would understand clearly.

"Is it like ordering a woman through one of your catalogues?" Brown Bear asked, finding the process very strange.

"No, Brown Bear. I am not ordering a woman. I am simply meeting eligible women from the East through writing letters." Mathew was trying his best not to laugh at the idea Brown Bear had pictured. "There are no women here in Bear Creek. I must meet women elsewhere."

Brown Bear thought about this idea for a moment, trying to see the problem from Mathew's perspective. Though he'd mastered the White people's language, there were still many customs that he did not understand.

"Very well, Mathew. You should begin your letters right away," Brown Bear said finally. "Tell all the women to come to Bear Creek so that perhaps the miners would be calmer." Mathew laughed hard with Brown Bear then. The words the older man sometimes said never ceased to surprise Mathew. Then, he grunted in parting as the man slipped back into the shadows.

Mathew tried to spot him in the fading light but the moment he stepped off the porch, Brown Bear melted into the dusk. It was one of the many things that Mathew admired about the Indians. They had amazing skills at being able to go undetected, even in the forest. Mathew certainly appreciated his friendship with him, and many of the other Indians.

After sitting for a while, Mathew finally rose from his rocker and went inside, calling Bailey after him. It was time he retired for the night, knowing that morning would come soon enough and the work of tending to the ranch still rested solely on his shoulders till he could earn enough to hire his own ranch hands. As Mathew readied for bed, he ran over his conversation with Brown Bear. He would certainly pay Sheriff Benning a visit the next time he went to town. But he also knew that if he truly did want to marry one day, placing a mail-order-bride ad would be his best bet.

After settling into bed with Bailey resting at his feet on the comforter, Mathew said his prayers. He prayed that one day things would be calm between the miners and the Indians. And that one night he'd be able to fall asleep next to his wife.

# CHAPTER 2

Jenny forced herself to keep breathing as she sat in the parlor with her uncle and mother. Four weeks had passed since the dreadful day she and her mother had had to leave their house, and though she took comfort in knowing that her father had been laid to rest in the church graveyard, each day afterwards had been an equal nightmare.

Where her father had been a kind man to Jenny and her mother, his brother was certainly not like him. It was no wonder that her grandfather had left the family business to her father. However, in the end the business had gone under whichever brother was in charge. Jenny did her best to push this trivial thought out of her mind as she focused on what her uncle was trying to tell her.

"Tonight, we shall dine with Mr. Prescott and his family. They have been kind enough to host us and have invited Mr. Miller, Mr. Daniels, and Mr. Canton in hopes of persuading one of them to give an offer to Jenny," Uncle Duke said as he spoke directly to his sister-in-law with barely a look at his niece. The woman he spoke directly to had become a ghost of her former self. Margret's skin was as pale as if she was sick all the time, and her eyes were often red and puffy from the excessive crying she could not help indulging in each morning and evening. Though she still kept her long black hair tidy, she was no more the beauty that Duke had found attractive in their younger years.

"But Jenny is only eighteen. These are all older men, almost twice her age" Margret replied with concern. Though Jenny would agree with her uncle that her mother still grieved heavily for her father, she would never openly agree with him on anything. Hearing the names of the men that Uncle Duke spoke sent chills of fear through her. The idea of marrying to preserve her way of life would have only been appealing if the gentlemen she was being thrown before were anywhere close to her age and had a decent reputation in town. But now that she had neither wealth nor reputation, the likelihood of her receiving a decent proposal was very limited.

"Considering the current position you two find yourselves in, *any* offer from *any* wealthy gentleman should be greatly appreciated regardless of their age," Uncle Duke said sternly. For a moment his eyes glanced towards Jenny as she sat in a chair near the window. Jenny thought his eyes were filled with disgust. She could only assume the man didn't like young people since he'd never married or had children of his own.

"Margret, your husband died bankrupt. Unless Jenny marries for wealth, you'll be looking for employment before long," Uncle Duke continued, his voice almost a threat. "You cannot live off my generosity forever."

The need to speak up threatened to overtake Jenny's sense of propriety. She longed to tell her uncle what she thought of him and shame him into giving her and her mother more leeway. But she knew that this type of outrage would not allow her to find a suitable place for her mother and herself. Jenny knew that they wouldn't be able to stay with her uncle for much longer. And after the papers had detailed why her father had shot himself before being allowed to be gunned down in the end, she knew that staying in Richmond was also out of the question. She couldn't very well find employment working for families she once considered her friends. It would be too much of an embarrassment for her and her mother.

"You have been very gracious, Duke. Please don't take my concern the wrong way. I just want to see Jenny in a good home when she is married." Margret looked to her daughter. Jenny could see tears in her eyes once more. For all the world, Jenny wished she could take her mother's pains away.

"If she doesn't marry soon, Margret, she won't have any place to call home." Uncle Duke rose from his winged-back chair and pulled his vest down over his protruding stomach, his muslin shirt barely able to stay tucked into his trousers. He then left the parlor room with a huff of discontent. Jenny was disgusted by the man. He was obviously well off by the way the sitting room was excellently designed with plush carpets and golden wall papers. But he would never lend a penny to a person in need. Though her father may have made some bad choices in his career, she knew that at least he had been a kind and considerate man.

With her uncle gone from the room, Jenny moved over to her mother and joined her on the settee. She took her mother's trembling hand in hers as she used the other to blot her eyes with the handkerchief that always seemed to be in her left hand. Jenny could smell the waft of peppermint on the collar of her dress as her mother did her best to keep her nerves calm.

"Oh, Jenny. Whatever shall we do?" Margret said in a soft voice. She was tired of crying but couldn't seem to do anything else. "I shall not see you married to an older man who simply can pay off your uncle for his permission."

"We will think of something, Mother. We need only keep our health up," Jenny said in hopes of comforting her. Margret only nodded and took several deep breaths.

"I don't like the idea of finding employment at my age, Jenny. It would feel strange to seek a position in a household when I am most likely acquaintances with them."

"Yes, I have thought of that myself. Though I'm sure it would be easy enough to clean house for another, I would find it dreadfully embarrassing to clean the room of a person that was once my friend." Mother and daughter sighed together as they sat on the settee, both trying to think of what they could possibly do about their situation. Though Jenny's mother had funds in her bank account, money inherited from her parents, it wouldn't last them very long if they decided to move out of her uncle's home. An apartment would not only cost to rent but also to furnish. Then there would be the expense of hiring someone to clean and cook. Jenny knew that they couldn't afford anything like that right now.

As Jenny sat with her mother, her gaze went to the paper on the oak table in front of them. Beside it their morning tea tray rested untouched. The idea had been to sit in the parlor for a time until Uncle Duke left for the day. But his announcement had rendered them both without another word to say. Jenny looked at the newspaper, remembering a time when she used to enjoy reading the gossip section with her friends. They would all gather for lunch and laugh over the outlandish things the reporters would find to write about. The more prestigious the family, the juicier the gossip seemed to be. But now that Jenny was certain that the gossip columns included her name, she wasn't eager to read the paper.

It was also in the paper that they had read the full report on her father's downfall. The day after her father had urged them from their home, Jenny and her mother had sat in the parlor, much like they were doing now, as Uncle Duke read the morning paper to them. Margret had sobbed as she listened, and Jenny had been stunned into silence, unable to move or feel. Her father had swindled many businessmen out of their money in hopes of saving his export business. But in the end, it had been discovered that all the money had gone to personal needs and wants. The business went under, the truth had been unearthed, and her father had made sure he was dead before he could be arrested.

Jenny shuddered at the memory as she turned her head away from her mother. She didn't want to show weakness or tears any longer and therefore did her best to keep her composure. After the incident, Uncle Duke had taken over everything that Jenny had considered hers. Her home and everything in it had been sold to pay her father's debts. She had very few personal belongings left. One memento that remained was a very small photo of her mother and father together when they had first been married.

"Do you want to be married, Jenny?" Margret asked her daughter, breaking the silence of the room and pulling Jenny from her deep thoughts.

She turned to her mother then, considering the question and the reason why her mother would ask such a thing. "Certainly I want to be married, one day. I just like the idea of marrying for love instead of convenience," Jenny replied. Margret patted her daughter's hand as she mustered up a smile.

"I, too, needed to marry for love. That is why I married your father," she said in a weak voice. Jenny smiled at her mother, knowing how much her parents had loved each other. "And I do want you to enjoy your husband's company, for when you marry a man, you spend a lot of time together."

"That sounds reasonable enough." Jenny was still unsure of what her mother was implying. Margret reached across to the table and picked up the paper. Jenny watched as her mother flipped through the paper until she came to a certain section. *Matrimonial Times* was the heading at the top. Jenny was surprised as her mother took the section out of the paper, tossed the rest away, and then moved so that both she and Jenny could read it.

"There seems to be respectful men who post ads in the paper," Margret said, drawing her daughter's attention to the section she had selected.

"If you can believe what they write." Jenny said as she held the other side of the paper and began reading some of the ads that had been placed. At first, she thought her mother was just playing a joke on her in hopes of lifting her spirits. She chuckled as she read out a few of them. "These men sound desperate for a woman to cook and clean for them. They aren't asking for a wife." But there were a few that caught her attention.

"Maybe it is something to consider," Margret said as she rose. "I am going to lay down for a bit," she announced as she made her way from the room.

As Jenny watched her mother walk unsteadily from the room, her heart seemed to drop even further. She hated to see her mother in such a state and wished beyond anything that she could take her from this home of dread and fear. Jenny focused back on the ads, wondering if she would have a better chance marrying a rancher or a cowboy. She had always assumed that she'd marry someone like her father. He would be a man who was kind, considerate, a businessman, and most importantly, handsome. The thought of marrying below her station, or even moving out West unsettled Jenny. How would she know how to handle such a situation? But as she looked up at the door through which her mother had just left, Jenny knew they had very little choice over their future now. She wasn't sure if she could satisfy the wants and needs of a rancher, but figured she'd have to give it a try.

Jenny returned to reading the ads. Perhaps this wasn't such a crazy idea. Might she be able to find one that offered her a way out of this dreadful situation she and her mother were in? Though she'd grown up desiring only friends of equal status and invitations to social events, could she learn to survive in the West and learn to do all manner of domestic house chores? She started to read with a new perspective, making mental notes of those she thought she might reply to, and silently prayed that if someone answered her letter, it would be a man who could rescue her and her mother.

 athew drove his wagon into town on a Friday afternoon. He didn't want to be gone from the ranch very long, but since the autumnal heat of the days had started to wear off, he didn't worry too much about his cattle. Nonetheless, Mathew always made his trips into town short and to the point. However, ever since he'd posted the mail-order-bride ad, he'd been frequenting town more often with the hope of receiving a letter in answer to his ad.

As Mathew held the reins in his hands, his eyes focusing on the dirt road ahead of him and his draft horse, he tried not to worry too much about finding a wife. He was a bit anxious and excited to receive a letter to his ad, but knew that it couldn't really affect his life as it sat now. He could go on about his business every day without having to answer to anyone or explain what he was up to. There was a sense of freedom that came with being a single man who managed his own property. But the more he tried to justify that he was fine on his own, the more Brown Bear's words seeped into his head.

"Why would any woman in her right mind want to come to a place like Bear Creek?" Mathew wondered out loud as he turned his wagon towards the small town. Buildings could be seen on either side of the road that led in and out of the town. Several store fronts lay empty, waiting for other business owners to move in. But ever since the gold mine had seemed to dry up, a lot of people had left town in a hurry with the idea of finding gold or other treasure somewhere else, or of simply living in a town that was thriving.

As Mathew drove the wagon up the main road towards Frys, the town's dry goods store, he thought the place looked fairly empty. Tibet's Inn rested to the left of him, a decent place to stay and grab a quick bite to eat. Mr. Tibet was a friendly owner, and Mrs. Tibet made the best peach cobbler. Sometimes Mathew would come into town when he got tired of fixing the same things for dinner and eat at the Tibets'.

Across from the inn was the small clinic managed by Dr. Harvey. He was an older man, someone that Mathew remembered from his childhood. Dr. Harvey was a stern fellow when it came to teaching others how to take care of their bodies, but he always had sweets for the children. Mathew often wondered when Dr. Harvey was going to take on an apprentice. He wasn't sure how much longer Dr. Harvey could stay in practice, and the thought only added to the gloomy thoughts Mathew had regarding Bear Creek.

Next to the inn was a barber shop, and as Mathew looked in the front windows, he was reminded once more about his need for a haircut. He was still indecisive over what he should do about it, even though he knew that Mitchel Franks was a great barber. He'd learned the craft from his father, and much like Mathew, had left school to take over the family business. Mathew knew it would be good simply to visit with his old friend, but he knew that Mitchel would cut his hair short in a heartbeat. Mitchel had a sense of fashion about him that sometimes Mathew found irritating. Especially when the broad-shouldered barber always critiqued what he wore into town.

Mathew was soon passing the barber shop and was able to see most of the rest of the town as the road curved to the right. Next to Mitchel's barber shop was the bank that was owned and managed by Louis Fritz. The eastern businessman had come out to Bear Creek when the town was booming with miners needing to cash out their gold. But when most of the miners left, so did Fritz's business. Mathew shook his head, wondering what the aristocrat was up to these days.

Pulling up beside Frys, Mathew tied the reins to the wheel peg as he put it into place to keep the wagon from rolling away. Mathew figured he'd just pop into the dry goods store to pick up some more flour when he saw Sheriff Benning walking down the street towards the Sheriff's Office. Needing to still speak to the man on behalf of Brown Bear, he followed after the Sheriff.

"Good morning, Jacob," Mathew said as he stepped inside. Deputy Williams was at his desk writing what looked like to be reports.

"Hey there, Mathew," Sheriff Benning hung his duster and Stetson on their usual peg and turned toward Mathew. "What brings you in?"

"Well, I spoke with Brown Bear not so long ago. He was telling me about the tension rising between his people and the miners. Says they are lighting dynamite close to his camp and scaring away all the deer," Mathew said. His words caused Deputy Williams to pause in his work as both men looked at Mathew with much concern.

"I swear that foreman is going to be the death of me," Jacob said with a sigh as he plopped down on his chair behind his desk. "I just rode in from the mine. Geoffrey was threatening to send word to the marshal if I didn't do something about the Indians bothering their operation."

Mathew's brows came together as he tried to imagine the Sioux bothering the miners. "What did Geoffrey say?"

"Says the Indians have been showing up in his campsite and trying to spook them away by making all sorts of animal sounds. Says it has the miners all spooked, and that Geoffrey doesn't have many miners left."

Mathew couldn't help but laugh over the idea. "Well, I won't say that it wasn't Brown Bear's people. Sounds like a few braves trying to play some jokes. Either that or Geoffrey is starting to get paranoid."

"Well, one thing for certain is that there aren't that many miners left. Geoffrey better find gold in that mine or he's not going to have any workers left," Tanner spoke up from across the room. Mathew and Jacob both agreed with the deputy as they continued to think about the matter.

"And now you're saying that they are using dynamite close to the Indian camp?" Jacob clarified.

"That's what Brown Bear told me. With them getting ready for winter as well, they'll be hunting and storing their supplies. Having their hunting grounds disturbed could lead to starvation for his people." The last thing Mathew wanted to hear about was people dying from another man's greed. Mathew could tell that his words were disturbing as Jacob looked at his deputy with much concern.

"Well, it seems that I need to have another conversation with Geoffrey. If he's working anywhere near the Sioux Indians, he'll end up provoking them." Jacob pushed himself to his feet, ready to take the necessary action to keep the peace in Bear Creek.

"And Brown Bear and his people will defend themselves if provoked," Mathew agreed.

"I better join you, Boss. We're dealing with a man who is already feeling pressure to provide results. It might be best if I spoke to him since I'm the one who has more tact than you do," Tanner said with a chuckle. Mathew watched as Jacob nodded in agreement before Tanner relaxed.

"That's why I pay you the big bucks, Deputy," Jacob said as he collected his Stetson and duster from the peg on the wall.

"Thank you, Jacob. This will mean a lot to both me and Brown Bear," Mathew said as he followed them out of the office.

Jacob locked the front door and said, "I simply don't want an Indian war on my hands, Mathew. I know you and some of the other townsfolk are partial towards the Indians. But tensions always seem to be rising." He then dipped his head, walked over to his horse and mounted, turning the beast towards the open road.

"We'll let you know how it goes, Mathew," Tanner said reassuringly before following his boss out of town.

Mathew sighed, hoping that a solution could be agreed upon. He, too, did not want to hear about the Sioux declaring war on the miners to preserve their way of life. Mathew knew for certain that if the Indians openly attacked the miners, it would only bring the army to town to drive them out or end their lives.

With a heavy heart, Mathew made his way over to Frys. Stepping into the establishment that doubled as the post station for mail and the stagecoach depot. Mathew said a friendly hello to the patrons before making his way to the front counter.

"Well, good day to you, Mr. Jenkins," Mr. Fry said as he stood behind the counter.

"Good day to you too." Mathew said as he shook hands with the older man. Though the Frys had owned the store since Bear Creek was first settled, the older couple were still friendly and active as always.

"What can I do for you today?"

"Just looking for a small sack of flour and wanted to see if any mail had come in today." Mathew pointed to one of the flour bags on the shelf behind Mr. Fry.

"Alright, here you go." Mr. Fry plucked the sack from the shelf and handed it to Mathew. "And let me just check the post box." Mr. Fry then picked up the large wooden crate of letters from underneath the counter and began flipping through them. Mathew watched, expecting Mr. Fry to find nothing for him. But Mathew was pleasantly surprised when Mr. Fry pulled out a letter and handed it to him. He was so surprised that he simply looked down at the letter for a moment.

"That will be thirty-five cents, Mathew," Mr. Fry said, pulling Mathew from his thoughts. He quickly pocketed the letter in his back pocket and pulled out a few coins for Mr. Fry. After paying the man, he picked up his sack of flour, said goodbye and quickly headed out of the store.

Mathew's heart was pounding as he placed the sack of flour in the back of the wagon, and then crossed the street to the church building.

As the main road wound to the right, that bend homed the large church building that also doubled as a town hall. Inside, he was sure that Mr. Dan Franklin would be there thinking of ways to bring more people to Bear Creek. He was a very dedicated man, and Mathew was thankful Bear Creek had such a passionate mayor. And from time to time, Pastor Munster would be in town. He was a traveling pastor and would give a sermon once a month at the church.

For now, Mathew simply sat on the shaded steps of the church and pulled out the letter. He looked down at the writing and saw that it was very elegantly written. He saw his name on the envelope and thought he'd never seen finer handwriting. Then, he read the writer's name on the back: Jenny Phillips.

"Well, Jenny," Mathew said to himself, "let's see what you have for me today." Mathew felt excited as he opened up what he assumed was his first mail-order-bride letter. He knew not to get his hopes up but did wish that this letter would offer a one-and-done situation.

DEAR MATHEW JENKINS,

I'm writing you from Richmond, Virginia. I found your ad in the Matrimonial Times and found it more alluring than most. You seem to be a respectful man who knows what he wants in life. My mother suggested I only reply to those who seem respectful, and I hope you are as true as your ad seems. I like to think that a man who manages his own ranch must be responsible, but also honest and reliable. These are qualities I look forward to seeing in my husband. As well as a man who is kind and considerate.

I feel that I also meet your requirements of a potential wife based on your ad. Though I am from the East, I don't mind the idea of moving to the West. I understand that life there requires more effort than the life I was born into. But you see, I'm a very determined person who always strives after what I want. And though I am young, just eighteen, I'm utmost concerned with securing a better future for myself, and my mother.

You see, my father ruined our family name by plunging his business into debt, swindling his investors, then avoided jail by killing himself. It's a very disheartening thing to write about, but it's no less the truth. As you require someone who is always truthful, I feel it pertinent to share all the details of my life with you. And now, my mother and I reside with my uncle. He is a very overbearing man who demands I marry the wealthiest man I can, despite age or reputation.

My mother and father married for love, and that is the kind of life I want for myself. I don't care about wealth or fine things. I want to spend my days with a man I can respect and trust. I'm in need of a place for myself and my mother as soon as possible. I'd like to come West as soon as I have a destination in mind. If you'd be willing to house my mother and I, I'd be willing to cook and clean for you. I'm not excellent in either task, but I'm willing to learn. I'm also willing to see if we'd be a good match. But if not, the simple idea of being out of Virginia is enough to have me packing and on the first train tomorrow.

If you agree to this arrangement, to allowing my mother and me to stay with you to see if we can be a good match, or until we can find lodging of our own once we've secured some sort of employment, I'd be willing to work for you. If you agree, send word to me straight away. I promise you won't regret rescuing me from this grave situation I am in. I'll even pay for mine and my mother's way from Virginia if I know we'll have a place to stay waiting for us.

My biggest hopes rest with you, Mathew.

Sincerely,

Jenny Phillips

BY THE TIME Mathew had finished reading the letter, he was certainly surprised. He'd never dreamed of receiving a letter of this magnitude and felt a solid weight had been placed on his shoulders to do something about Miss Phillips situation. With the letter, Jenny had also included a photo of herself. Though black and white, the photo showed a beautiful young lady with a strong disposition. She looked straight at the camera, a hint of a smile on her face. She looked as determined as her letter had described her to be. And there was a certain fieriness that caused Mathew to smile since it was coming from a young lady who'd been born into wealth.

After folding the letter back together, Mathew sat for a moment and looked toward his horse and wagon. A part of him wanted to return home and give himself a few days to think about the matter. He wasn't sure that allowing a young lady and her mother to stay with him was such a good idea. It might be frowned upon by others in the community. And since Bear Creek was such a small town, he knew that gossip would spread like wildfire.

But as Mathew thought of the pleading way in which Jenny had written her letter, he knew that he couldn't ignore her, either. Mathew knew that there weren't a lot of young ladies in Bear Creek, and certainly not as beautiful as Jenny. He knew that if he didn't reply to her as soon as possible, he would have both a guilty conscious and perhaps leave a woman in what seemed to be dire need.

Mathew got up from the steps of the church and crossed the dirt road to Frys. He reasoned that having Jenny and her mother come to Bear Creek would at least increase the number of eligible women. He didn't expect Mrs. Phillips to remarry after losing her husband so suddenly, but he knew that the possibility was at least there for other members of his community. In the end, he figured he was doing a great service to Bear Creek as he entered Frys and went back up to the counter.

"Did you forget something, Mathew?" Mr. Fry asked, the same kind smile on his face.

"No, sir. I simply would like to purchase some writing paper and perhaps borrow your quill. I must write a letter, and have it posted immediately," Mathew explained.

"Well then, it will cost you to borrow my quill." Mr. Fry chuckled. Mathew knew the man was only joking, but he played along, nonetheless.

"If you insist, Mr. Fry," Mathew replied as he took the material that Mr. Fry handed him. Mathew's response to Jenny's letter was short and to the point. He encouraged Jenny and her mother to come straight away to Bear Creek. That if nothing else, he'd help them get settled in a community that was very friendly, and greatly in need of women. After finishing his letter, he folded it up and addressed it.

"Here you go, Mr. Fry. Thank you for your assistance." Mathew handed Mr. Fry the letter and paid him for posting it.

"Always glad to help, Mathew," Mr. Fry replied as Mathew made his way out of the store once more.

The weight that had seemed to be placed on Mathew's shoulders drifted away as he pulled himself back onto the wagon. After removing the peg from the wheel and securing the reins in his hands once more, he turned the wagon around and made his way home. He felt good about writing the response letter before leaving town. He thought it was awful what Jenny was going through and couldn't imagine what it must be like to be forced to marry someone. Even if she and Mathew didn't decide to get married, Mathew could think of five or more other gentleman that might be interested.

But as Mathew made his way out of town, he surely hoped that he'd find Jenny as fierce and passionate in person as she appeared in her letter and photo.

# CHAPTER 4

Jenny was fuming on the inside as she walked circles around the pristine gardens at the back of her uncle's large home. She'd just turned away her third marriage proposal after being happened upon by the suitor in the drawing room. She hated how often these men would find her unaccompanied in the house; it made her think that her uncle had designed it that way. But even though Jenny had been alone, she wasn't going to allow these men to pressure her. No matter how much they were willing to pay her, or her uncle for his permission.

Jenny felt disgusted to be preyed upon by these men. It was her life after all, and even though her uncle would no doubt be furious with her for denying yet again another suitor, she wouldn't allow his wrath to sway her decision. She still had hope in her heart that soon she'd find a way to leave this place behind. Jenny just kept reminding herself that she only had to be patient.

"Miss Phillips," came the voice of her uncle's housekeeper. She turned to face Honey, the former African slave that her uncle still treated as such. The woman handed her a letter, no expression on her face. Once the letter was in her hands, the plump woman turned and walked quickly back inside the house.

Jenny stepped behind a towering rose bush. She looked down at the letter in her hands, rough handwriting having sketched out her name. But she was able to see that it was from Mathew Jenkins. Her heartbeat sped up as she quickly tore it open and read the very short message. She read it a dozen times before she held it firmly in her hands and raced inside the house.

"Mother! Where are you?" Jenny called. There was no reply, so Jenny took to the stairs. As expected, she found her mother in her room, simply sitting on the edge of her bed as though she had been waiting for something.

"What is it, Jenny?" Margret asked, fear coursing through her as she looked up into her daughter's happy face. She certainly wasn't expecting Jenny to be in this state and wondered if she had accepted the odious suitor's proposal. But a letter was thrust into her hand.

"I've received a response from a Mathew Jenkins who lives in the West, in Montana, far away from here. He's given permission for us to come and stay with him. That we may become settled in Bear Creek till we can find our own way," Jenny explained, her chest rising and falling as she did her best to catch her breath.

Margret read over the letter, her mind spinning over the words. She hadn't realized that Jenny had answered one of the mail-order-bride ads, and was even more surprised that a complete stranger had agreed to house them. Could she really leave behind all that she'd ever known? Though her closest friends had abandoned her after her husband took his life, could she make new friends in Bear Creek who were more loyal and compassionate?

"What are the man's terms?" Margret asked as she handed the letter back to her daughter. Though the idea was appealing to finally have a reason to leave Richmond behind and all it's horrible memories, she wasn't going to allow anyone to take advantage of her beautiful daughter.

"I've offered to clean and cook for Mr. Jenkins in return for shelter for both you and I."

Margret raised an eyebrow at her daughter. "But you have no idea how to keep house. We were never trained to do domestic housework."

"Certainly it cannot be that difficult," Jenny reasoned as she came to sit next to her mother on the edge of the bed. "I shall purchase instruction manuals when we go out shopping. I've always been a quick learner and you have a keen eye for food. Your dinner parties have always been the best because of the menu you'd construct for Cook."

"And why on earth would we go shopping? Your uncle will not lend us any money, and I don't want to spend any from our savings till we know what we are doing." Margret had to really consider her daughter and what situation they could find themselves in once moving to Montana. The territory had still not become an official state, there were horrible news reports about Indian attacks and other such crimes, and how did anyone uphold the law in such an untamed place? And furthermore, would they come to miss the ease of living in Richmond? It was a civilized town with plenty of resources.

Yet, she had not seen Jenny this happy in a long time and wished she could feel the same. She'd been so oppressed by Duke; the way he behaved towards her filled her with dread. He'd insisted, threatened even, that Margret should stay in her room so a suitor could propose to Jenny without her interrupting. She had a hard time believing that their life would be anything other than this nightmare if she stayed in Richmond any longer.

"Mother, you must withdraw all your money from the bank. We shall then purchase our train tickets once the route has been mapped out for us and then purchase necessary things we will need. Then, we shall simply leave this dreadful place behind forever," Jenny said happily. She started calculating in her mind the amount they had in the bank, the cost of the trip, and where they should go to shop for the things they'd need. She was so lost in thought that she jumped when her mother placed her hand on her shoulder.

"Are you sure we should do this, Jenny?" Margret asked her daughter carefully. "This is not a light matter to discuss."

Jenny knew that for a long time her mother had been afraid. It didn't help that the love of her life had taken his life, leaving his family in complete ruin. Jenny didn't even try to imagine how her mother must have felt through all this. She simply couldn't leave her to suffer any more.

"Mother, I will not allow you to remain in this house any longer. Uncle Duke is a ghastly man who will more than likely die an old and lonely man," Jenny said without regret. "I will not leave you here to deal with him. We shall leave for the West immediately since there is nothing left in Richmond for us."

Jenny's confidence seemed to spark a sense of hope in Margret that she hadn't felt since her husband took his life and destroyed theirs. The idea of leaving behind everything she'd ever known was frightening in and of itself. But the thought of Jenny being forced to marry a horrible man, and for herself to have to work for one of the families she used to host dinner parties for, was a harder future to face. Therefore, she placed her hand in Jenny's and squeezed.

"Alright then, Jenny. Let us go prepare for our grand journey to venture West and meet this Mr. Jenkins," Margret said, trying to seem as confident as her daughter. "And you never know. Perhaps you'll come to love the man."

Jenny chuckled as she squeezed her mother's hand back. "I doubt that will happen, Mother. But if Bear Creek is really in need of young ladies, then I am sure to meet someone who can capture my heart." Then together, mother and daughter left the house to put their plan into action.

IT HAD BEEN a week after Mathew had posted his letter to Jenny when he found himself in the pasture daydreaming about the young lady. He often thought of Jenny, knowing that it was certainly possible that she and her mother would soon come to Bear Creek. If she was as desperate as she sounded in her letter, then Mathew was facing the reality that he'd be meeting this lady and her mother soon. Sometimes the thought brought dread to Mathew, influencing him to clean up the house a bit and get the two spare bedrooms ready. And other times it brought so much excitement to Mathew that it seemed to course through his body. It had been a while since he'd tried his way with a woman, and the idea of getting to court Jenny, a beautiful young lady, made him eager to meet her.

His daydreaming was interrupted as a horse came galloping towards him in the pasture. Mathew raised his hand to his brow to shield the sun from his eyes so he could get a good look at the man that was fast approaching him. The familiar Stetson and duster gave him away as Sheriff Benning came into sight. Mathew was surprised to see the Sheriff at his home and hoped that the man wasn't bringing him bad news.

"Afternoon, Mathew," Jacob said as he slowed his horse and then pulled up beside him. Bailey came scurrying over as he barked happily to see a visitor. Mathew shushed him, wanting to know what had happened.

"Afternoon, Jacob. To what do I owe this pleasure?" Mathew asked. The stern expression on Jacob's face told him that this wasn't going to be a pleasant visit.

"I've spoken with the foreman, Geoffrey, about the dynamite, and the man didn't seem pleased that I was bringing it up," Jacob explained. "Then he produced some sort of land deed that shows he owns the land that the Indians are on."

Mathew felt like the wind had been forced out of his lungs. He was immensely surprised by the news and couldn't fathom how any of this could be true.

"The man has to be lying, Jacob. If it was true, he would have forced the Indians off his lands years ago when he first opened up the mines." Mathew's temper was quickly rising. He didn't like the idea of anyone taking advantage of Brown Bear and his people. He also didn't like the idea of his friends having to leave the area.

"Trust me, Mathew, me and Tanner have discussed all the possibilities. But Geoffrey has threatened to push the Indians off his land himself if I don't do something about it," Jacob explained, his expression darkening. "But I've given the deed to Louis Fritz since he's an expert at these things."

"That's a good idea, Jacob. As soon as Louis proves it's a fake, you can nab Geoffrey for forgery and get him off Brown Bear's back," Mathew said with a nod.

"That's the plan, Mathew. But till then, I'm going to need you to come with me so I can discuss this with Brown Bear. He deserves to know what is going on, and the possible outcome of Louis proving that the deed is not a forgery." A cold chill passed over Mathew then, and it wasn't because of the cooling weather. He didn't even want to imagine what it would be like for Brown Bear and his people to relocate. There was less and less available space for Indians to remain safe from White people's influence.

"Fine, I'll go with you, Jacob. Just let me do the last of my rounds and we can go right away."

"I'd appreciate it, Mathew," Jacob replied as he dipped his head. Mathew clicked his tongue, sending his horse into a fast trot as he circled the herd. Mathew gave Bailey his orders to round up the herd and keep them together by whistling high and long. Though his eyes were making sure that there was no way for the cattle to escape the pasture while he was gone, his mind was racing over the possible outcomes of this meeting.

Brown Bear had always been the diplomatic type. That is why after Mathew was able to deter the miners from attacking the Indians during their hunting party, he and Brown Bear had quickly become friends. Mathew was impressed with Brown Bear and enjoyed spending time with the Indians because he had no family left of his own. He thought very highly of the Indian's way of life and would have gladly joined Brown Bear's tribe if he didn't feel so connected to his father's ranch.

Mathew hated the idea of having to tell Brown Bear that another man might own the land his people currently lived on. He could already predict Brown Bear's confusion over this idea since his people had lived in the same spot for hundreds of years. As Mathew made his way back to Jacob, who was patiently waiting for him, Mathew said a silent prayer that he'd be able to speak the words needed to help Brown Bear and his people.

"All ready then?" Jacob asked once Mathew returned.

"As ready as I'll ever be," Mathew replied. "Bailey, watch over things while I'm gone. Stay home boy," he said to his trusted cattle dog. Bailey sat back on his hind legs, waiting for his master to return. Mathew then led Jacob from the pasture, and together they headed West of Mathew's property. Up into the hills they went, following a familiar trail. But the closer they came towards camp, the more Mathew was filled with uneasiness.

# CHAPTER 5

As Mathew rode into camp with Jacob right behind him, he smiled at familiar faces, nodding as he weaved his horse through the teepees. When he reached the horse corral, he dismounted and tied the reins of his horse to a hitching post. Jacob followed suit, and as soon as they were ready, Mathew led the way to Brown Bear's teepee.

Reaching the Chief's teepee flap, Mathew scratched his fingers against the bison hide and waited for permission to enter. Instead, they were soon greeted by Brown Bear. He looked delighted to see Mathew at first, but when his eyes settled on the Sheriff, his expression soon turned serious. He knew that Jacob was the town's sheriff and hoped that none of his people might be in trouble with the White man.

"Hello, Brown Bear. I've come to speak to you about a troubling matter," Mathew said. "You remember Sheriff Benning, don't you?"

"Yes, Mathew. Hello, Sheriff Benning. Welcome to my home," Brown Bear said with a gesture for the men to join him in his teepee. Brown Bear held back the flap and ushered the two men inside. Mathew always found it interesting how much room was inside a teepee when it appeared small from the outside. It was considerably warmer inside as well as a small central fire burned within, the smoke rising and escaping out of the top hole of the teepee. Mathew sat down next to the fire on a mat, pointing to the mat next to him for Jacob to join him.

"Thank you for inviting me inside your teepee, Brown Bear. I feel it is suitable since I have something sensitive to share with you," Jacob said as he got settled on the ground. Mathew tried not to smile as he watched Jacob try to get comfortable. It was obvious to him that the Sheriff wasn't used to being on the ground.

"Please, go ahead, Sheriff. I am all ears, as you say." Brown Bear sat and crossed his legs, leaning forward on his elbows as he peered at Jacob over the fire.

"Brown Bear, I have taken the time to speak with Geoffrey, the foreman of the miner's group," Jacob started. "I went to see him after Mathew explained to me that the miners had been using dynamite close to your camp and had startled the deer away."

"Ah, I see. Thank you, Sheriff, for speaking on behalf of my people. I would speak to this Geoffrey myself if I didn't fear an altercation." Brown Bear was pleased to hear that his words to Mathew had been heard and that this official of the White man had spoken for him. But Brown Bear was certain that there was more to this story.

"I agree with you there. I, too, don't want any sort of trouble up here," Jacob said. "But after I spoke with Geoffrey about where he was using dynamite, he then gave me a piece of paper that was very startling." Jacob looked at Mathew then, hoping his friend would back him up after he spilled the beans with the Indian Chief. "You see, Brown Bear, Geoffrey has what's called a land deed. It explains ownership of a particular piece of land."

Brown Bear grunted then as he straightened his back and crossed his arms over his chest. "Forgive me, but the idea of owning land is very offensive. The land is free to all who live upon it and it should be respected so."

"I understand your traditions, Brown Bear, and think your views are amicable," Jacob said, trying to placate the Chief. "But it doesn't help the fact that Geoffrey has a document that states he owns the land that your tribe is currently occupying."

Mathew and Jacob went silent for a moment while Brown Bear slowly processed what Jacob had said. Mathew watched as Brown Bear's eyes narrowed at Jacob, then him. It was an unsettling sight and Mathew could only imagine that his friend was battling an internal war against his feelings of anger.

"Sheriff Benning, how is it possible that a man should own the land that my people have occupied for several generations?" Brown Bear asked carefully, wanting this to be a productive meeting. He did his best to control his feelings over the matter so a solution could be discovered. Though he'd rather gather his warriors to wage war against the miners to protect their lands, he knew in the long run that this solution would not be productive.

"The government of the White people has given people the opportunity to claim land that has been previously unclaimed by settlers," Mathew spoke up, wanting to explain it in terms that Brown Bear would more easily understand. "It seems that Geoffrey claimed this land the camp is on, and all the land in the hills surrounding it in order to mine the hills for gold."

Brown Bear grunted once more as he shook his head. "We were here first, long before White man was known to us. I should have been given this land paper as I am the leader of these people." Brown Bear was very confused. How anyone could own land when they did not live on it?

"I understand how puzzling this all may be. But please be rest assured that we have someone making sure that this land paper isn't a fake," Mathew added, trying to give Brown Bear some hope over the situation. "If it is a fake, then Sheriff Benning will be able to arrest Geoffrey and shut down the mine."

Brown Bear smiled at this, thinking it would be nice to be rid of the miners once and for all. "But how can I purchase the land my tribe is on in order to avoid this problem in the future?" Mathew sighed, knowing that the answer the sheriff would have to give would be another issue entirely.

"Brown Bear, Indians cannot purchase or own land unless they pledge to become American citizens and assimilate into White culture. The Dawes Act of 1887 is what started to allow Indian tribes the opportunity to have land in exchange for becoming US citizens," Jacob explained, already knowing that Brown Bear would never do such a thing. When Brown Bear growled in return, a chill ran down Jacob's spin. His instinct was to reach for the pistol on his hip, but he knew better than to move a muscle and spook the Chief even further.

"Perhaps someone else could purchase the land, a White person who could then make a deal with the Sioux Tribe?" Mathew spoke up, wanting to cool Brown Bear's feelings over the matter. Brown Bear and Jacob both thought of this idea, both trying to imagine how this informal proposal would work out.

"First we have to find out if Geoffrey owns the land or not. And if not, we'd have to contact the state to figure out how to secure this land and what the procedure would be," Jacob explained. He looked to Brown Bear then as he said, "We don't want any trouble. My deputy and I will work with your people to find a solution."

Knowing that no more could be done for the time being, Brown Bear grunted his approval. "Let this matter rest for the moment." Then, he gestured to the opening of the teepee. "Would you two care to join me and my tribe for the evening meal?" Jacob was surprised by the Chief's hospitality, thinking the man would be too angry to spend any more time with White people.

"I would enjoy that very much, Brown Bear. Thank you," Mathew said, giving Jacob a pointed look that warned him it would be impertinent for the man not to accept as well.

"Yes, Brown Bear. Thank you," Jacob quickly added.

"Very good. Let us move to the central fire pit." Brown Bear stood and left the teepee. Mathew and Jacob both stood and followed Brown Bear through camp. Jacob had to admit that something smelled good as he watched several Indians gathering around a large fire that was in the center of their camp.

"You did good in there," Mathew said in a soft voice as they found an empty spot on a log to sit and wait for the maidens to finish preparing the meal. Jacob sat down, glad to have something to sit on besides a mat as he watched the maidens fish clay pots from deep within the hot coals of the fire. As lids were lifted, the air was filled with a savory aroma.

"Thank you, Mathew. For a second, I was sure Brown Bear was going to declare war to protect this land," Jacob replied in a whisper.

Mathew chuckled as he looked at Brown Bear as he sat on the other side of the fire. He was sure that the Chief was explaining the situation to the elders of the tribe.

"Brown Bear is a good leader. He does well to put his feelings aside to think of the greater good of his people," Mathew said. "Much like you would do to protect the town of Bear Creek." Jacob nodded in agreement. He'd always taken his position as sheriff very seriously and was ready to protect the settlers no matter what.

"I just hope I can fulfill my promise and make sure there isn't an Indian war in these hills." Jacob was offered a wooden plate with what looked like roasted venison with root vegetables and a brown gravy. He looked at the food with much curiosity and then tried to work out how to eat it as he thanked the maiden.

"Let's hope that Louis finds that the deed is a fake," Mathew said as he accepted a wooden plate and began eating right away. He knew he needed to get back to the ranch before nightfall so that Bailey wouldn't be out in the pasture all night.

"So, I'm guessing there are no forks." Mathew looked at him as he licked his fingers. Mathew grinned and shook his head.

"Eat with your fingers or wait for the basket of nom bread to be passed around so you can use it to scoop up the food. I'm too hungry to wait," Mathew explained before digging in.

Jacob chuckled as he followed his friend's example. "You know, Mathew, if you keep growing your hair long, people are going to mistake you for a half-breed." Jacob had to admit that the food was delicious and that eating with his fingers wasn't the worst thing he'd ever done.

"Yeah, I keep thinking I need to pay Mitchel a visit. At least get it trimmed," Mathew agreed. "And I should probably do that sooner than later."

"Oh yeah? Is there a particular lady you're hoping to impress?" Jacob asked as he ribbed Mathew with his elbow.

"Hey, cut that out," Mathew said as he moved out of Jacob's reach. "And yes, there is a young lady that I am hoping to impress." Mathew didn't give Jacob any more details as they finished their meal, taking a few pieces of nom bread to mop up the gravy and ensure their plate was clean before giving it back to the maidens.

"So, spill it, Mathew. Who's this girl? Surely no one around here." Jacob was dying to know where Mathew had met someone because there were no eligible women in Bear Creek. It was a fact that sometimes kept him up at night as he tried to figure out how he ever was going to get married.

"I got this idea to place a mail-order-bride ad during the cattle drive to the auctions. Met a fellow there who told me all about it and how he met his wife," Mathew explained, feeling a bit silly to be telling his friend about what he'd done. But he figured that it was honestly the only way anyone in Bear Creek was going to find a wife.

"So, are you saying that you did this? That you placed an ad for a bride?" Jacob asked, certainly not expecting Mathew to tell him this.

"Well yeah, Jacob. I sure did," Mathew said as a proud smile grew on his face. "In fact, I think she and her mother will be showing up in town before too long."

"Seriously? She's coming out here with her mother?" Mathew then took the time to explain the entire situation to Jacob as his friend silently listened till he was done explaining everything. Jacob instantly felt for Jenny and her mother. He couldn't imagine what it must feel like to be so hopeless and desperate, or to be forced into marrying someone you don't love.

"I see then," Jacob said when Mathew had finished talking. "Well, I do agree with you that this town could use more women. And if she and her mother would be willing to do some housekeeping work, I'm sure others in the community would appreciate it. Just imagine how happy the Frys would be to have an extra hand."

Mathew chuckled as he thought about the older couple. "Yeah, I'm sure they'd appreciate it. I just don't know if anyone can pay them. Not a whole lot of money coming into this town as of late."

Jacob nodded as he looked all around him. He was surrounded by friendly Indians who were able to make or gather all that they needed. Unfortunately, the people of Bear Creek relied on the flow of money to make ends meet.

"It's something I think about every day, Mathew. And I'm sure Mayor Franklin does, too." Jacob stood and brushed the dirt from his jeans. "Well, I best be getting back to the office. Tanner is going to want to know how this meeting went."

"I'll lead you out and show you the trail that heads straight back to town," Mathew said as he stood as well. After saying goodbye to Brown Bear and thanking the maidens who had cooked for the tribe, Mathew led Jacob back over to their horses.

After showing Jacob the way back to town, Mathew turned his horse and followed the trail down the hill and through the forest to his ranch. As the sun was setting with hues of blue and fiery oranges filling the Montana sky, Mathew hoped that things would be resolved between the Indians and the miners. Even more so, he hoped that Jenny and her mother were doing okay. He couldn't wait to meet them both.

# CHAPTER 6

The rocking of the train thundering down the tracks was a soothing sound to Jenny. It meant that with every minute that passed, she and her mother were that much further away from Richmond and the grasp of her horrible uncle. Jenny knew that Uncle Duke wouldn't waste his money coming after them, but until she was settled in Mathew's house, Jenny was certain that she wouldn't be able to relax fully. Jenny watched the scenery pass by the train windows, thinking how beautiful the country looked as tree leaves had turned to shades of yellow, orange, and red.

Preparing for this trip had been much harder than Jenny would have ever imagined. It had taken a lot of research to discover which trains would travel West, in what cities and towns they'd need to change trains to reach Bear Creek, and lastly finding out at which train stop a stagecoach could be hired to take them the rest of the way since the train didn't run anywhere near the remote Montana town. Planning their travel arrangements alone had proved to be a large puzzle that Jenny and Margret had to put together by speaking with the train station attendant in order to finally travel with confidence.

By her side on the train, her mother sat with a cookbook in her hands. It was one of the few personal items they had decided to bring with them. And since Jenny had finished reading it after three days traveling by train, it was now her mother's turn to enjoy it. Jenny was hoping that once her mother finished reading it, they could trade it for another at one of the many train stops or during the times they'd need to stay overnight in a town while they waited for the next train to take them further West.

As they had prepared for this trip, Jenny and her mother had quickly learned how to purchase things that were more affordable than their usual purchases. Their traveling gowns had been purchased from a secondhand store. Jenny had never bought anything used before, and she was certain her mother hadn't, either. And despite their initial doubtful thoughts of used clothing, they had pushed them aside to buy the things they thought they'd need for this trip and living in the West. Jenny had chosen a plain gown in a burgundy color. She was certain it would both be comfortable, but also hide stains well for when she was certain to be working.

"This looks like a lovely recipe," Margret said to her daughter as she pointed down at the book. Her finger rested on a recipe for a shepherd's pie that Margret reasoned wouldn't be too difficult to replicate with the detailed instructions.

"Indeed, Mother. It says that almost any vegetable could be used in the recipe. I guess it just depends on what is in season," Jenny said, reading the recipe through. Though Jenny had never cooked for herself in her life, she was more confident after having read the cookbook from cover to cover.

"Perhaps when we arrive in Bear Creek, we can make it for Mr. Jenkins," Margret suggested, feeling happy to have something positive to look forward to.

"I think Mr. Jenkins would love that very much. Certainly cowboys enjoy hardy meals such as that," Jenny agreed happily.

When they had snuck away in the night to meet the train, Jenny hadn't been certain how her mother would fare on the trip West. It would be almost two weeks before they reached Montana, and another three days by stagecoach before they'd arrive in Bear Creek. It would be a long journey, there was no doubt in that. And since traveling could be very tiresome, Jenny had feared how her already weak mother would handle the long trip.

As the days passed as they traveled, Jenny seemed to see her mother come alive for the first time since her father had taken his life. Color had returned to her complexion, even when the only things they had to choose from to eat were cheese, salted meat, and bread. Her mother never complained when it was hard to find fresh foods to eat or how uncomfortable it was to fall asleep on the train. They didn't have a compartment of their own, and so they slept in the passenger car with everyone else.

"When in Rome, do as the Romans," her mother had said as they learned to be comfortable aboard the train. They slept with their heads angled towards one another as they leaned back into the train seats. They walked carefully up and down the cars to get daily exercise. And though it was an almost frightful experience to use the toilets on the train when it was just a seat over a hole, Jenny had done what was needed. She found it all very surreal and sometimes it added to her fear of leaving behind the only place she'd ever known. She'd never traveled outside of Richmond before and sometimes doubted her abilities to live and survive as a settler in the West. But seeing her mother almost happy again gave Jenny the strength she needed to keep a cheerful disposition.

As Jenny focused her attention back on the scenery, she started to think about Mathew. She prayed that he was as kind as his letter had led her to believe. Though she wouldn't be able to judge his character until they were properly introduced and able to spend time together, she simply prayed that she wasn't leaving one bad situation to go running into another. Jenny did her best not to think negatively and remain positive that her future was heading in the right direction. Though she was doing something she would have never imagined for herself just two months earlier, Jenny was determined to succeed and find a better home for her and her mother.

Jenny then turned her mind to what it must be like to live in the West. She pictured wide open spaces that one could look at all day and never see the end of. She prepared herself for the fact that Mathew's home was no doubt much smaller than the eighteen-room home she'd grown up in. Jenny was doing her best to stay as realistic as possible. Even the train depots had given her a sense of what life was like outside the big city of Richmond. Though Jenny didn't have to worry about any one's opinion but her own, and of course her mother's, she did have to keep an eye open for any possible danger.

There was so much to keep in mind when it came to traveling and no doubt living in the West. Instead of sending someone to the grocer for dinner, she'd have to gather supplies herself and cook her own meals. There would be no dress shops and she would have to figure out how to keep her gowns nice or perhaps order something from a catalogue. Maybe there would be a dressmaker in Bear Creek? Jenny sighed then, knowing that there were so many unknowns still yet to be discovered.

Jenny turned her head to look at her mother once more. How desperately she wanted this trip to be successful. Though Jenny had put very little thought towards marriage, or the idea of marrying Mathew, she was at least willing to do whatever it took to see her mother happy once more. It would be hard for both of them to find employment and learn the skills necessary to be self-sufficient, but they truly had no other choice. Jenny refused to marry someone she didn't love just to live a comfortable life. She took a deep breath as she thought of countless wishes. She simply needed to be settled and safe in a home with her mother once more.

"Do you think we could learn to make strawberry tarts?" Margret asked, pulling Jenny from her deep thoughts once more.

"I don't see why not," Jenny replied. "Cook always made the best tarts." Jenny smiled at the memory as her mother looked over at her.

"Indeed, she did. If only I had paid more attention when she made them," Margret said, a sad tone seeping back into her voice.

"There will be other women in Bear Creek who could possibly

share with us their favorite recipes," Jenny said as she tried at every opportunity to encourage her mother. Margret nodded as she flipped the page.

"Can you imagine, Jenny? We'll have to learn to ride horses and grow our own garden," Margret said, a bit uneasy.

"How wonderful, Mother. I have always liked horses. I shall ride one so fast that I'm certain to give you a fright," Jenny said as she laughed, making her mother chuckle with her.

"My goodness, I do hope you will not do anything so reckless," Margret replied once their mirth had subsided.

"Of course not, Mother. But the idea was a humorous one," Jenny said as she patted her mother's hand. "Well then, I shall go to the dining car and see what they have for a simple lunch."

"Alright, dear. If by chance there is a strawberry tart, I think it would be a nice treat to share one with lunch," Margret said as Jenny slowly rose from her seat and stepped into the aisle.

"Sure, Mother. I shall ask the attendant," Jenny replied with a smile. She took a few coins from their shared purse, then made her way towards the door that she could slide aside to make her way to the back of the train where the dining car was. It would be good exercise for her, but also give her a moment alone to collect herself.

Sometimes, she felt proud of what they were able to accomplish together. With just two small trunks between them, they'd fled her uncle's home without the need or want to return. There was a sense of freedom that Jenny was able to feel as the train pulled out of the station and took them far away from everything that plagued them. But even though they'd escaped a certain horrible future, Jenny only hoped that what lay ahead of them would be ten times better than what they faced in Richmond. Either way, Jenny was certain that she'd never travel back to Virginia.

# CHAPTER 7

*M*athew did his best to keep his nerves under wraps as he stood on the front porch of Frys. After receiving a telegram from Jenny that she and her mother were expected to arrive in town on the stagecoach today, he had done everything he could think of in preparation for their arrival. Mathew had even convinced himself to finally get a haircut. Even though the ends of his brown hair still reached to right above his shoulders, at least it wasn't down the middle of his back anymore.

So many thoughts and ideas ran through Mathew's head as he paced back and forth on the front porch. He hoped that Jenny and Margret had traveled well. Mathew could only imagine how exhausting traveling for two weeks had been. He assumed that they would be in want of rest and planned to treat them to lunch after collecting their things from the stagecoach.

And even though Mathew knew that Jenny's main priority had been to come to Bear Creek to start a new life with her mother, he'd also taken the time to shave and wear his best shirt and jeans. He wanted to look good for Jenny with the hopes of perhaps impressing her enough to consider official courting. Mathew knew that he would respect whatever boundaries Jenny put in place. Since, though, the two of them would be staying on his ranch, there was a part of him that still hoped that their relationship could lead to a happy marriage.

As Mathew looked down the road leading out of town, he saw a dust cloud lifting into the air as a stagecoach rumbled down the road. He stopped dead in his tracks as he focused his attention on it, the moment had finally come. In just a few minutes he'd come face to face with Jenny and her mother, making his heart beat hard against his chest. The stagecoach was being pulled by a six-horse team that was causing the stagecoach to fly across the road. The driver was very alert as they entered the town, causing him to slow down his team to stop on time in front of the dry goods store.

As the stagecoach came to a stop Mathew took a deep breath. The driver hopped down from his seat and quickly unlatched the door before removing several items that had been strapped onto the back. Mr. Fry came out of the store then, eager to see what supplies had come to town while Mathew kept his eyes on the carriage door. Then, when it was finally opened from inside, Mathew caught his first glimpse of Jenny.

Mathew couldn't help but smile as Jenny's bright face came into view. Slowly, she stepped down from the stagecoach, her auburn hair catching the afternoon sun. It seemed to glow, even though she had done her hair simply in a braid. Her traveling gown was also simple, not something Mathew would expect a socialite from Virginia to wear, but it didn't detract from her beauty. She helped her mother down from the stagecoach then, the older woman wearing her long black hair loosely. Though older, she was still a beautiful woman, and Mathew saw where Jenny got her good looks from.

Knowing the time had come, Mathew stepped off the front porch and greeted the women. "Good afternoon, Mrs. and Miss Phillips I presume. I am Mathew Jenkins," Mathew said as he approached them.

Jenny turned from her mother at the sound of someone addressing her. As she made eye contact with his hazel eyes, she quickly saw the most handsome man she'd ever laid eyes on. Back in Virginia, there had been few gentlemen that had caught her fancy, but none of them compared to Mathew. He was tall with longer brown hair than she'd ever seen on a man before. His shirt hugged his torso in a way that led her to believe that the rancher was very strong. His legs seemed to go on forever as she noticed his jeans. She'd only ever seen men in trousers and found the sight very alluring.

"Good afternoon, Mr. Jenkins," Margret spoke up when she noticed how distracted her daughter had become. She couldn't help but smile as the two young people regarded each other for the first time. She could see appreciation in both of their eyes and wondered if anything would ever become of it.

"I hope you two have traveled well these past two weeks," Mathew said as he tore his eyes from Jenny's and regarded Mrs. Phillips. He saw the way she smiled and wondered what she made of him. He wanted to impress her as much as her daughter.

"It was an adventure for sure," Jenny said, finally finding her voice. "We learned so much simply by riding the train that perhaps we are a bit more prepared for Montana living."

"All the people we met along the way were so very lovely," Margret added. "Such friendly folks that it was like taking a breath of fresh air. Though, I am excited about making a homecooked meal."

"You two make riding the train sound almost enjoyable," Mathew remarked, surprised by their positive disposition. He certainly wasn't expecting how chipper they appeared.

"Well, I wouldn't recommend it if you can avoid it. Practically living on a train for two weeks isn't for the faint of heart," Jenny said, glad to know that she more than likely would never have to ride a train again. That thought alone allowed her to have a brighter outlook on her life. She then began to glance around, wanting to learn all she could about Bear Creek.

"Well, ladies. Let's get you settled. I'll place your trunks in the wagon and then I thought I could treat you to lunch," Mathew said as he gestured to his wagon. Jenny and Margret looked at it, both looking curious but optimistic.

"Lunch sounds lovely, Mr. Jenkins," Margret said as the driver pulled their trunks down from the stagecoach. With Mathew's help, their things were collected and stored safely in the wagon. Margret wasn't eager to get back on the road, so she was pleased to hear that they could rest for a moment.

As Mathew approached Jenny and offered her his arm, Jenny couldn't help but blush. She gladly allowed him to lead her down the boardwalk with her mother close behind. She was certainly pleased that Mathew had some gentleman like characteristics.

"Bear Creek is a small community, but there is enough in town to satisfy all your wants and needs. There is an inn that has a decent menu. Mrs. Tibet is a wonderful cook and makes the best peach cobbler in town," Mathew said as they walked together. "Here is the bank, owned by Louis Fritz. And past it is a barbershop. Then is the inn that is managed by Mr. and Mrs. Tibet."

"I did not expect Bear Creek to have a bank," Margret spoke up as she looked through the windows. The place seemed to be empty, even though a man stood behind the counter. She knew she'd need to deposit her money but wondered if she should just keep it with her instead. After all, she'd managed to keep it safe during the last two weeks they'd been traveling without any issues.

"Bear Creek was founded on mining, Mrs. Phillips. Louis opened the bank to give miners a place to cash in their gold," Mathew explained.

"Understandable," Jenny said as she looked up at Mathew. "Is mining still a major part of the community's economy?"

Mathew was impressed by Jenny's question. He wouldn't have expected a young lady to be interested in such things. "Not like it used to be. Though the mine is still active, it hasn't produced any gold in a long time. Most miners moved away to go find gold elsewhere, but there are a few that have remained in the hopes of striking it rich."

"Then what is the main commerce of Bear Creek now?" Jenny asked as she looked around. She spotted a medical clinic across the way, along with the largest building in the town that appeared to be a church of some sort.

"Well, there are several ranches outside of Bear Creek, along with a handful of farms. There are a few businesses in town as well. I would say that's about it," Mathew explained. He'd never really thought of it himself and found Jenny's perspective very enlightening.

Mathew led them inside the inn and towards the dining room that had a few patrons inside. Once being settled down at a table near the window, Mr. Tibet came over to greet them. He was an older gentleman with graying hair. But his blue eyes twinkled with delight to see new people in town. Always dressed in his best pair of jeans and a freshly pressed western shirt, Mr. Tibet was always ready to greet customers and patrons to the inn.

"Afternoon, Mathew. Always good to see you," said the older man. "And who are your guests?"

"Mr. Tibet, I'd like to introduce you to Mrs. and Miss Phillips. They've just come into town and I wanted to treat them to lunch," Mathew said as he gestured to the women.

"How lovely. It's a pleasure to meet you," Mr. Tibet said as he dipped his head towards them. "Mrs. Tibet has made a lovely shepherd's pie this morning, as well as a meatloaf."

"I shall love to try the shepherd's pie," Margret spoke up excitedly. "I did read about it in a cookbook during our travels and would love to experience the dish."

Jenny chuckled at her mother's enthusiasm. "And I shall try the meatloaf so that we can both try a bit of each," Jenny said.

"Meatloaf for me, Mr. Tibet," Mathew said as he did his best to refrain from laughing. He could tell that Mr. Tibet was perplexed that the women hadn't tried these dishes before, but he wasn't willing to explain their background. In a small town, one couldn't be careful enough with what information they shared with others.

"I must admit. I didn't expect to meet two cheerful women this morning after traveling so far," Mathew said once Mr. Tibet had left them.

Jenny smiled kindly at Mathew as she thought about her words before speaking. "After what we left behind, Mr. Jenkins, it is easier for us to feel happiness," Jenny said.

"I agree with my daughter. There is a whole new world ahead of us and I believe we are both excited to experience what life has for us now," Margret added to Jenny's wise words.

"Well, I'm certainly happy to see you both well and here in Bear Creek. This small community could benefit from two beautiful women such as yourselves," Mathew said with a genuine smile. Jenny and Margret chuckled together. Mathew could see the blush in Jenny's cheeks as she averted her eyes from him.

"You are too kind, Mr. Jenkins," Margret said. She was used to such flattery and could handle the compliments well. But she could clearly see the blush in Jenny's checks. She found it amusing as she turned her gaze back to the young man. "We may be a little road weary, but we found the area quite lovely. Such wonderful wide-open spaces. You certainly don't have to worry about peeking neighbors."

Mathew chuckled at the idea. "Well, homes are spaced out here. Most live out of town and travel in when they need something," Mathew agreed. "But this is still a small community where everyone's business seems to get passed around easily enough."

Jenny nodded, knowing that the same thing happened in Richmond. "It is no different than rumors and gossip being shared about other families in town. It's a bit exciting to hear what is going on in other people's lives," Jenny admitted as she remembered how she used to love gossiping with her friends. "But I think there is a certain type of gossip that shouldn't be repeated." The last thing Jenny wanted was Mathew to think she was a busy body and concerned more about the business of others instead of her own wellbeing.

"I can agree with you there, Miss Phillips. It's good to know how others are doing, but never wise to speak ill of anyone," Mathew said.

"So glad you understand," Jenny replied with a smile. A moment later, Mr. Tibet returned with their food. Though the plates were much simpler than the porcelain Jenny had been used to all her life, she ignored that fact and simply focused on the food. A square cut of juicy meat lay before her on the plate with a brown gravy covering it with a large helping of mashed potatoes. Though it was foreign to Jenny who was more used to French cuisine, she couldn't deny that it smelled amazing.

"Looks delicious," Margret said to Mr. Tibet as she looked down at the slice of pie. It was filled with meat and vegetables, and a buttery sauce pooled from it.

"Please give our compliments to Mrs. Tibet," Mathew added. He was finding it amusing how delighted the Phillips women seemed to be with their food. Though it was common food to him, their reaction made it seem more appealing than usual.

As they ate, Mathew watched as Jenny and Margret took bites of each other's food, commenting on the tastes and textures. They both seemed eager to replicate the dishes and wondered how they would go about gathering the ingredients. Mathew found it all very amusing and was starting to feel good about his decision of inviting them both out to stay with him while they got settled. Perhaps it was the type of company he'd been missing in his life. If they were this interested in their food, he couldn't wait to hear their opinion of his childhood home.

"There is a butcher in town where you can get your ground beef and pork. I keep a meager garden but there are still some carrots and potatoes that could be dug up before the first frost comes. But with winter right around the corner, simple dishes can be made like biscuits and some sort of meat gravy," Mathew said.

"From what I've been able to read, meals from dry goods and canned items are more popular during the winter when fresh ingredients are less attainable," Jenny said, hoping to impress Mathew with her knowledge. Now she needed the experience to bring her ideas to reality. She knew she would need to cook for herself if she was going to survive. As she looked down at her empty plate, it dawned on her that this was probably the last meal she'd have cooked for her in a long time.

"You would be correct, Miss Phillips," Mathew said with a kind smile. "Things will certainly be different for you here in Bear Creek, but not impossible."

"Certainly not, Mr. Jenkins. You have done well on your own," Margret stated. "I know you'll have much to teach city women such as ourselves."

"And there are others in the community who'd be willing to teach you as well. I'm sure Mrs. Tibet would be thrilled if you asked her for lessons," Mathew said.

"Then we will be certain to inquire of her assistance in the future," Jenny said, her hopes rising that they wouldn't be alone in learning all these new skills.

After Mathew had kindly paid for their meal, Jenny and Margret followed him back to his wagon where he helped them both up onto the driver's bench. "It's a bit cramped up front, but better than riding in the back," Mathew said with an apologetic look. But as he came around to the other side, close to Jenny, she wasn't put off at all. She enjoyed being so near him and seeing everything around them from this perspective.

"How far is your home from town, Mr. Jenkins?" Margret asked as Mathew collected the reins and urged his horse into a trot as they made their way out of town. Margret held firmly to the edge of the wagon, fearing that she might fall if they hit a large bump in the road. Jenny noticed her mother's uneasiness and placed a reassuring arm around her.

"Not that far, Mrs. Phillips. I understand that the two of you must be quite tired, so I shall urge Danny to keep a fast pace," Mathew explained as he flicked the reins once more, causing the draft horse to pick up speed.

Jenny found it thrilling to feel the speed of the wagon rolling down the open road. In the stagecoach, it had been hard to see much of anything out the small window. Now Jenny could feel the wind in her hair and smell the fresh air of the countryside. As the town disappeared from view, wide open spaces stretched out as far as she could see. It was as though the open land could kiss the horizon in the far distance. To the right was a forested area that grew on the sides of several hills. They seemed to form some sort of mountain in the distance and Jenny could only imagine that the miners lived up in the hills where they tried to dig for gold. Jenny didn't like the idea of being underground and hoped that she'd never have to be inside a mine in her life.

After a while, Mathew steered the horse down a lane. A small ranch home came into view as Jenny caught first sight of Mathew's home. It was a one-story house with a large front porch. The outside had been stained in dark hues, but the many windows made it appear inviting. Smoke rose up from the chimney and Jenny couldn't wait to see inside. Also on the property was a decent sized barn and several pastures that were framed by a fence. As they neared the house, Jenny could smell the distinct aroma of cattle. It wasn't entirely unpleasant, but it reminded her she was no longer in Richmond.

"What a beautiful home," Margret said as the wagon came to a stop in front of the ranch house. They had arrived and she was looking forward to getting some rest soon. Mathew came around the wagon and helped her down, followed by Jenny. And the moment Margret stepped onto the front porch, a collie came bounding over from the barn, barking excitedly at the women.

Margret was uncertain about the dog, never being fond of them, but Jenny bent down and petted the dog in greeting. The collie licked Jenny on the face a few times before wandering over to his master in greeting.

"Behave yourself, Bailey. We have guests," Mathew told the dog as he retrieved the trunks from the wagon. Then, he led them inside the house as Bailey sat on the porch and waited for his next order.

Jenny was pleasantly surprised by the design of the ranch house. The center of the home had a dining table that was worn with age as though it had hundreds of stories to tell. It didn't compare to the polished mahogany table that used to reside in her home, but Jenny didn't want to compare this modest ranch house to what she used to have in Richmond. It would only bring down her hopes and that was the last thing she needed.

On the far wall to the left was the chimney where a small fire burned with a large iron fire grate in front of it to keep the coals contained during the day when Mathew was not around to keep an eye on it. The back housed the kitchen with a woodburning stove that had two open ports for heating pots on top and a narrow oven for bread making. A dry sink was all that was available for dishes and Jenny was reminded that running water was a rare commodity in Bear Creek. She'd have to learn to do things much differently than what she was used to. Jenny caught sight of a pantry and was curious about what she would find. But she made sure to keep an eye on Mathew as he led them down a narrow hallway to where the bedrooms were.

"I've made both rooms for you to use. Feel free to decide between yourselves who is having what room," Mathew said as he set down the trunks and opened the doors for them. Jenny was surprised by the way he easily lifted their two trunks, showing just how strong he was. Jenny smiled kindly at Mathew as she stepped into the first room with her mother. It was simple with a bed in the center and a dresser with a water basin resting upon it. Blue lace curtains framed the window that gave a perfect view of the cattle pastures in the front.

"Jenny, I think this room would be perfect for you," Margret spoke up since the other bedroom was closer to the third bedroom at the end of the hallway. Margret assumed that was Mr. Jenkins room and she did not like the idea of Jenny sleeping so close to a man's quarters.

"I agree," Jenny replied. Jenny then pulled her trunk into the room and set it down at the foot of the bed. Margret did the same with hers as she went into the other bedroom.

"Well, I'll let you ladies get settled. I'm going to head out and check on the cattle and ensure the fences don't need any repairs. I should be back about the time the sun is setting," Mathew said as he looked at both women as they took in their surroundings. He was pleased to see that they had pleasant expressions on their face as they took everything in. He could only imagine that his home lacked many of the luxuries they were used to and could only hope they'd come to enjoy this home as much as he did.

"Thank you, Mr. Jenkins. We shall see you after a bit," Margret replied, pleased to have a quiet moment with her daughter. Margret watched as Mathew nodded towards Jenny and then left the house. They heard him whistle to Bailey as he made his way towards the barn.

Jenny went to her mother in her room and looked around. It was similar to her own and Jenny thought it was lovely enough. The idea of sleeping in a real bed seemed very pleasing. And though the rooms were not as fine as the guest bedrooms in her home in Virginia, it was plenty spacious enough for them. Jenny spotted the chamber pot underneath the bed and was instantly reminded that things were very different in Bear Creek. She hadn't used one of those since she'd been young and fallen very sick once, too weak to make it to the water closet.

"What do you think, Mother?" Jenny asked softly, trying to remain positive. She could see the weariness in her mother's face and was concerned about her.

"I think it will do, Jenny. There is plenty of space here, even though the home is modest," Margret replied as she looked around. She thought that the room could use some uplifting touches such as brighter curtains and perhaps a rug on the wooden floors. But then she reasoned that such things were harder to come by in this remote part of Montana. Margret knew that there would be some things about Richmond she would miss, and she was doing her best not to miss anything about that dreadful place.

"Well then, how about you rest for a time. I'm going to peek around the main part of the house and see what I can discover in order to start making some sort of meal for dinner. There must be a few hours till sunset and that shall be time enough to make something."

Margret chuckled as she looked at the bed longingly. She hadn't had a proper rest in so long and she looked forward to resting on a real bed again. "I'll leave the task up to you, Jenny. I shall join you after a while."

Closing the door to her mother's room, Jenny walked down the hallway to the main part of the home again. She thought it was rather cozy, though lacking a woman's touch. She could imagine seeing a vase of wildflowers on the dining table and perhaps a fresh coat of paint on the walls. If they were white, Jenny figured, the space would feel more open and refreshing. But then Jenny reminded herself that this wasn't her home. She was only going to be staying here till she and her mother could find a place of their own.

But as Jenny made her way to the pantry, curious to see what supplies were available, she wondered if perhaps this home would one day be hers as well. She couldn't deny that Mathew was a very handsome man, and very kind. He'd shown them both the utmost respect and didn't show any signs of foul play. Even being so far from town, Jenny didn't fear staying in Mathew's home. Instead, she could feel love radiating from its walls because it had been so well maintained.

However, Jenny probably wasn't the type of woman that Mathew would want as a wife. After all, she lacked any experience when it came to cooking and cleaning, she wouldn't know the first thing about riding a horse or driving a wagon. At that moment, Jenny doubted herself very much if Mathew would ever consider her suitable. Eventually, Jenny had to push those negative thoughts out of her mind. They'd arrived in Bear Creek to escape the past tragedies. Now, they had to make the most of life and create a home they could both be proud of. And none of that was dependent on Jenny marrying.

# CHAPTER 8

As Mathew rode in from the pasture, looking forward to putting Daniel in his stall for the night, he was eager to learn what the Phillips women had been up to during the past afternoon. Mathew was thankful that none of his cattle had wondered off, and he was certain that Bailey had played a big part in keeping the herd together.

After making sure that Daniel was taken care of and the cattle had plenty of water in their troughs for the night, Mathew finally made his way inside with Bailey by his side. It was a hassle to bring in water from the creek that ran alongside his property to the east, but he was at least glad he had a water source on his land. The first thing Mathew realized was that a savory aroma was coming from the kitchen. As he took off his boots by the door since they were covered in dirt, Mathew saw Jenny and Margret milling about in the kitchen, laughing between themselves.

"Oh goodness, I think I've burnt them," Margret said with a chuckle as she removed a cast iron pan from the small oven compartment. She set it on top of the stove as both women leaned over it, poking at the raised dough.

"Nothing a little butter won't fix," Mathew said as he came around the table to see what they had been trying to make.

"The idea was to make stuffed rolls with salted meat and vegetables and served with a tomato sauce I've steeped over the fire," Jenny explained as she removed the lid from her tomato sauce. Though it looked a little dark, Mathew reasoned that it couldn't possibly taste as bad as it looked.

"I can't wait to try it." Mathew's words didn't match his expression, but he was trying to reassure both of them that they'd done well for trying cooking for the first time.

As Mathew washed up after fetching a pail of water from the well behind the house, he then helped set the table. It was almost a surreal feeling as he sat down at the table with the women, a homecooked meal before him. It reminded him of the days when he'd come in from working with the cattle with his father, and his mother would have food waiting for them on the table. Mathew could feel tears pricking his eyes as the memory came to mind, but he was quick to force the emotions away as he started filling his plate.

"You have a very lovely home, Mr. Jenkins," Margret said as they ate. She found that the food didn't taste too bad, even though the tomato sauce was very bitter. It lacked the sweetness that she was used to and made a mental note to look up the recipe once more from the cookbook.

"I'm glad you think so, Mrs. Phillips. My grandfather built the home when he and my grandmother first settled here. My father added onto it when he married my mother with the hopes of having a large family."

"You are an only child then?" Jenny asked as she tried the food. She knew that it wasn't that great and felt even more determined to work on her cooking skills in the future. After all, if she didn't learn to cook at least decently, she was worried that Mathew wouldn't agree to house them any longer. They had a bargain and Jenny needed to keep up her end of their deal.

"Yes, that is correct," Mathew said with a hint of sadness in his voice. Jenny noticed and wondered how lonely Mathew must have been living in this house all alone. Well, almost all alone. She saw how Bailey sat by his master's feet, waiting patiently for a bite of food.

"Douglas and I also wanted a large family. But since the birth of Jenny was so difficult, we didn't dare try again," Margret said, trying to smile at the memory. Every time she was reminded of her husband, a sharp pain seemed to spread across her whole body. It took great effort to force it away.

Their conversation seemed to drop into silence as they finished their food. Mathew then showed them how to haul water from the well as Margret carried two candles for them to see clearly. Margret wasn't used to such darkness as she looked around. No other house was in sight, and except for the moon and stars, there was very little light to show the way. She felt much more comfortable inside as they carried in two buckets of water to take care of the dishes and to use for self-washing before readying for bed.

"It seems this day has finally come to an end," Margret said as she handed Jenny one of the candles. "I'm going to retire for the night. Thank you, Mr. Jenkins, for such a warm welcome."

"It's my pleasure, Mrs. Phillips. Rest easy," Mathew said with the dip of his head. He watched then as the older woman went down the hallway with her candle and pitcher of water.

"I'm just going to get these dishes cleaned up," Jenny said as she went over to the dry sink. She set the candle on the counter and put the stopper in the sink before adding a small amount of water to scrub the dishes clean. Jenny wasn't used to the work, but she was willing to learn.

"Let me give you a hand," Mathew offered as he picked up a towel, ready to dry them off.

"Thought I would insist I do it myself so I can both learn and hold up my end of the bargain, but I am so exhausted that just this once I think I'll accept the help," Jenny said as she washed a plate, then handed it to Mathew to dry and put away.

"Sometimes it's easier if you do things together," Mathew said with a shrug of his shoulders. Jenny simply smiled as she familiarized herself with the dishtowel and a bit of bar soap. It took some time to get everything clean by the dim light of the candle, but she was thankful for Mathew's company while she did so.

"First thing in the morning, I plan to rise early and get to work around here," Jenny said, not wanting the silence between them to become uncomfortable. "Just give me an idea of what you want done besides breakfast and lunch."

Mathew thought about it for a second. A part of him didn't want to give her a to-do list, but he had a feeling that Jenny's pride would get in the way of him trying to refuse her services. After all, they did have a deal.

"Well, there is a chicken coop at the back. You probably didn't see it in the dark, but you'll hear the rooster in the morning. That's a good place to get eggs," Mathew explained. "A bit of tidying up could be used around here. I'm gone most of the day and don't usually have the extra motivation to clean when I get home." Mathew felt a bit sheepish to admit these things, but being honest was very important to him.

"I think Mother and I can find our way with the chickens, as well as a mop and soap. You might be surprised what you think of the place when you get back." Jenny gave Mathew a positive smile. Mathew couldn't deny that he enjoyed seeing her smile. She had some of the most beautiful blue eyes he'd ever seen on a woman, and they seemed to sparkle when she smiled.

"I like your positivity," Mathew admitted. "I wouldn't have guessed you'd be so excited about housework. I would assume instead that you'd be desperately missing Richmond right about now."

"Well, despite what you might think, this beats what Mother and I just left behind. Not only was my uncle a ruthless man, but Mother and I never felt up to leaving the house unless my uncle forced us to attend some dinner party," Jenny explained. "We couldn't bear to show our faces in public, and therefore my uncle's house became like a prison for us."

"I can't imagine what that must have been like for you two," Mathew said in hopes of comforting her.

Jenny sighed as she thought about it all. But then she smiled. "Coming out here has given us a sense of freedom. We managed to get all this way on our own and are able to go and do as we please without us worrying what other people will think or gossip about us," Jenny said happily. "It makes me wonder what else we are capable of."

Mathew chuckled as he dried the next dish and put it away. "You're starting to sound like a strong, independent woman. That's the type that does well out here in the middle of nowhere," he said. "You have to learn to take care of yourself and rely on the community when you do need help. For example, harvest season just finished. I used to spend my mornings helping the local farmers bale hay in exchange for some hay for my horse and cattle. I then store the hay in the barn so I can keep the herd fed during the winter."

"I like the idea of being a part of a community instead of just living in some town where I only have a few close friends," Jenny said, thinking about it. Though she had known many people in Richmond, none of them seemed to be her true friend after the news hit the papers. She'd been swiftly abandoned by everyone she'd known. But if the citizens of Bear Creek had to rely on one another, then perhaps she didn't have to fear about her new friends leaving her one day.

As she watched Mathew from the corner of her eye, she was starting to see how respectful and responsible he was. It was a characteristic she hadn't really seen in another gentleman and couldn't deny that he could possibly be a good match for her.

"Well, I bet everyone in town is eager to meet you and your mother. In a few days I'm sure we could make another trip to town," Mathew suggested. "You'll have to learn to drive the wagon eventually and that would make for good practice."

"Oh my, I can't imagine driving the wagon. I'm still contemplating the best way to wash these dishes."

Mathew chuckled as he finished drying the rest of the dishes and putting them away in the cupboard. "Like most things in life, Miss Phillips, don't overthink it too much," Mathew advised.

"Mr. Jenkins?" Jenny spoke up then as she pulled the stopper out of the sink and let all the dirty water drain out and collect in the bucket underneath.

"Yes?" Mathew asked as he turned his attention to her.

"You don't have to call me Miss Phillips. You could call me Jenny," she explained with a kind smile. Mathew returned the gesture as he nodded.

"Well then, you must call me Mathew in return."

"It's a deal, Mathew," Jenny said, saying his name slowly for the first time. She liked how it sounded on her tongue, and as she looked at Mathew with just the glow from the candlelight on him, Jenny couldn't help but think him rather handsome.

"Well, I suppose I should show you a few things about the pantry and the meat safe outside," Mathew said as he set the damp towel on the side of the sink to dry. Though Jenny had found many ingredients in the pantry that matched the cookbook she'd brought from Richmond, Mathew helped her identify the rest of the supplies in the pantry before taking her outside to show her the meat safe.

"One is all I need for a year," Mathew explained. "In the fall I have Curtis Denver, the local butcher, come out to the ranch to butcher two of my cattle. Whatever I don't use, he gets to keep for his shop as a thank you for helping me with the job. I salt the meat to preserve it and keep it in the meat safe." Mathew opened the small box while Jenny held the candle out, seeing the different cuts of meat as Mathew pulled back the cheese cloth covering them. He explained to her what the different cuts were used for, how the roasting pieces were the ones with the bone left in and the ones that had been already cut into small pieces were used for stews.

"I would like to try my best at using these cuts for a roast or a stew." Mathew gave her a reassuring smile before he shut the box once more, showing her how to make sure it was secure so no animals, especially bears, could get into it. Then, he took her back inside to finish showing her around the kitchen.

"I try to keep an active amount of yeast in the pantry to make bread on Sundays to tide me over for the week," Mathew explained. "If we ever run out of yeast, I do have a small amount of baking soda that can be used as a substitute, unless you want to try your hand at sourdough bread." Jenny wrinkled her nose at the idea, having tried sourdough bread and not having enjoyed the experience.

"I'll make sure to keep an eye on the active yeast in case more needs to be made or purchased. The idea of a fresh loaf of bread on the table for dinner is such a comforting thought." Mathew shrugged his shoulders as he yawned. He didn't mind either way but was now starting to feel exhausted as well. It had been a long day full of all sorts of excitement.

"The morning always comes so quickly," Mathew said as he finished yawning. "It's about time we retire for the night."

"Sound advice," Jenny agreed. She looked around the house once more as she picked up the candle from the counter. There would be plenty to do in the morning and for now she could use a good night's rest.

"Sleep well, Jenny," Mathew said in parting as he led Bailey down the hallway towards his room. Jenny just nodded as she watched him go, disappearing into the shadows of the house. When she heard the door close, she made her own way to the spare bedroom. Behind the closed door of the room, Jenny let out a deep sigh. She set the candle on the nightstand and began undressing in order to wash up.

Using the little bit of water from the basin sitting on the dresser, Jenny did her best to wash herself thoroughly. How she longed for a nice long, hot bath. She wasn't sure if Mathew had a tub, or how hot water would be obtained, but she mentally put it on her list of things she wanted to discover. Though she understood that many of the things she was used to in Richmond wouldn't be easily accessible in Bear Creek, she was still determined to obtain some of the creature comforts that she was used to.

After cleaning and dressing for bed, Jenny blew out the candle and then crawled underneath the covers. Though it wasn't as comfortable as her bed in Richmond, she was simply thankful to be able to lay down and stretch her arms and legs. She had a room of her own, and Jenny reminded herself that she had much to be thankful for. And as her eyes drifted shut, she smiled at the handsome image of Mathew.

THE ROOSTER'S morning call pulled Mathew out of a deep sleep. The chill of the night had set into the house and Mathew disliked the idea of getting out of bed when it was much warmer under the covers. But as Bailey made his way from his feet to his head before licking him on the face, Mathew relented and quickly moved from the bed.

"I'm up, I'm moving," he reassured Bailey as he started to pull clothes on over his long johns. With a light jacket on and boots over his wool socks, Mathew ventured from his room with Bailey close on his heels. As he went down the hallway, he glanced at the two spare bedrooms. It appeared that both women were still asleep, and he reasoned that was a good thing. Though they had been in happy dispositions yesterday, Mathew could only imagine how exhausted both of them had felt but refused to let on.

Wanting to get out into the pasture as soon as he could to see how the cattle had fared overnight, Mathew quickly built up the fire in the central fireplace to heat the ranch house. Then, he went over to the stove and added a few more logs before lighting the fire. With the coffee kettle on, he waited for the water to boil so he could make his morning cup of coffee. He wasn't sure if the Phillips women were used to coffee, but figured they'd enjoy the gesture, nonetheless. It seemed they were easy enough to please despite once being very wealthy.

After snacking on a bit of cheese and salted meat while he waited on his coffee, giving Bailey bits of his meat, he looked out the front windows to see the morning sun rising. He smiled, thinking it was going to be another great day on the ranch. He enjoyed his work and took great pleasure from it, and the thought of having company warmed his heart. It felt good to know that at the end of the day he'd have someone to look forward to talking to. Though he loved his cattle dog and took much comfort from the collie, it did not make up for human interaction. He was also curious to see how the Phillips women would fare after a whole day to themselves.

When Mathew finished preparing his coffee, he settled down at the dining table. Already the house was warming from the open fire and with the stove properly heated he only hoped that the women would keep the fire tended or it would grow chilly in the house once more. Before too long, winter would be in full swing and even snow would start to fall. Montana winters could be brutal, and he hoped to teach the Phillips women a thing or two about winter survival.

But for now, Mathew had to get to work. After finishing his cup of coffee, he placed his tin cup in the sink and headed out the front door with Bailey on his heels. The chilly morning air greeted him, causing him to wrap his arms around his body as he walked out to the barn. Once Daniel was saddled, Mathew rode out into the pasture to see how the cattle were doing on this particular chilly morning.

The pasture grass was covered with frost as the morning sun sparkled off it. Bailey ran ahead of him, excited to wake up the cattle and get them moving. The cold weather months meant that Mathew had to keep the cattle moving to stay warm. Bailey's excited barks sounded ahead of Mathew as he led the draft horse at a trot. Small clouds of steam rose up from the cattle as they huffed, their warm breath rising in the air. Mathew smiled, knowing that this chill was nothing compared to what would soon come. Mathew knew that he needed to make headway with his winter storage. But as he started moving the herd around the fenced pasture for their morning exercise, Mathew's thoughts were more occupied with Jenny. He smiled, looking forward to seeing her that afternoon.

～

THE MORNING SUN shone its warming rays through Jenny's window, waking her. She rolled away from the light and realized how stiff and sore her body was from all the traveling she'd done, and the chill in the air didn't help, either. As she breathed a sigh, she even noticed her breath misting in the air. She sighed, knowing that it was one more thing she had to learn about living in the West. She knew that it became colder in Montana than it did in Virginia and had made sure to purchase warmer garments for such weather. She simply hadn't realized that she'd need to use them so soon.

Jenny sat up in bed just as a knock came to her door. "Come in," Jenny called, assuming that it was her mother. As Margret popped her head through the door, she smiled happily down at her daughter.

"My dear, you're not going to believe where the toilet is," Margret said with much amusement in her voice. Jenny was surprised to see her mother up early and already dressed for the day. She'd pulled her hair back but let it flow down her shoulders in a cascade of black tendrils.

"I had forgotten to go looking for it last night," Jenny admitted, her own bladder protesting for waiting so long to go. "I had only seen the chamber pot and wasn't thrilled at the idea of using it."

"It's in the little house outside," Margret said with a chuckle. "After I could not find it inside, I went outside and saw it about thirty steps away from the main house."

"With how chilly it feels, I don't look forward to going all the way out there," Jenny said as she pulled the covers back up and over her body. "But it would be better than having to use a chamber pot and then dealing with it later."

"Don't worry, it's much warmer in the main part of the house. The fire has been built up and I reason Mr. Jenkins has already gone out this morning," Margret explained as she opened the door fully. "I'll leave this open while you get dressed so it warms up in here, too."

"Alright. I'll be out in a moment and you can show me this outside toilet," Jenny said with a shake of her head as she got out of bed and quickly dressed in a day gown with cotton undergarments. Deciding to wear her traveling boots instead of house slippers if she was going to be in and out of the house all day, Jenny then braided her auburn hair before making her way into the main part of the house.

"Mr. Jenkins left a pot of coffee on the stove for us," Margret said from the kitchen as Jenny met her. Jenny agreed that the central room felt much warmer. She looked towards the fireplace and was happy to see that there was a stack of wood beside it. Now all she had to do was remember to put logs on if the day continued to remain cold.

"I'll try some coffee after I use this toilet," Jenny said.

"Well, let me show you then," Margret said with a smile. After heading out the back door, they were able to see things much more clearly in the morning light. Jenny took care of her business, disliking the idea of having to go out to the toilet during the cold months. But knowing that it was the way of the West, she didn't let it discourage her from enjoying her first full day in Bear Creek. Relieved, Jenny joined her mother Margret as they then entered the chicken's pen in their attempt to collect eggs.

"They seem friendly enough," Jenny said as she slowly entered the hen house. The chickens clucked as they curiously neared the women, pecking at the hem of their dresses before moving into the yard. When all the chickens seemed to be out of the way, Jenny poked her head into the coop.

"The smell is quite unpleasant," Margret said as she fanned the air in front of her nose.

"That is an understatement, Mother." Jenny laughed as she quickly collected the eggs from the nests and then showed them to her mother. "I bet if we give them a good wash, they'll taste fine."

"I do hope so. I could use a good breakfast," Margret said as she helped Jenny hold up her skirt to provide a way of carrying the eggs. It was slow going for them, but eventually they were able to wash the eggs and crack them over a warm skillet with a bit of lard in the pan. Jenny found a small satchel of salt and seasoned them as she mixed them together in the pan. Margret discovered a loaf of bread and cut a few slices before buttering them and placing them on the table. Lastly,

Jenny collected a few buckets of water from the well, thinking they'd come in handy throughout the day. They had two full cups of water to go with their meager breakfast as they sat down at the dining table to eat.

"Well, it certainly looks edible," Margret said before taking a bite of the eggs. She then chuckled as she spit out a bit of the eggshell that had managed to make its way into the pan.

"Oh goodness, Mother. I am so sorry," Jenny said as she began to laugh. "I guess I should be more careful."

"It tastes fine," Margret replied as she took a bite of the bread and butter. "I think we should try our hand at baking fresh bread today."

"Indeed. I think fresh bread would be a nice addition," Jenny said as she tried the food as well. It wasn't horrible, but nowhere close to what they were used to. Jenny reasoned that eventually she'd be able to make tasty dishes like Cook used to for her family. She simply congratulated herself as a sense of accomplishment for making her own breakfast as she turned her thoughts to the rest of the day.

"We should try to wash our clothes today, Mother," Jenny said when they had finished eating. "Mostly everything I brought I've worn getting here."

"Yes, that would be a good idea," Margret agreed. "I'm sure there is a wash bucket around here and I saw a bar of soap at the sink last night." Margret had been educated on all the ins and outs of housework when it came to instructing her servants. Though she had the knowledge, she'd never tested it before since she'd never had a reason to work for herself. But she figured that if she could manage a household and all the work needed to maintain a manor or put on a successful dinner party, then she and Jenny could figure out how to do the work themselves.

"Well, I'll try my luck at washing if you want to see about putting that loaf of bread together," Jenny offered. "If I remember correctly, bread needs to rise for a time before it can be baked."

"Oh yes, the active yeast aspect," Margret said as she remembered the details of the bread recipe from their cookbook. "I'll read the recipe once more before I get started."

Jenny smiled as she collected their plates and set them in the sink. She then poured her and her mother a cup of coffee before sitting back down at the dining table once more.

Passing her mother a tin cup of coffee, she said, "I do hope we'll come to enjoy living here. I like to think it won't be all hard work every day."

"Though there is much to do, Jenny, I think that having work isn't all that bad of an idea," Margret reasoned. "It will keep us busy and will not allow our minds to wonder so much and reflect on things of the past. Though I'm sure there will be times when we can do leisurely things."

Jenny thought about her mother's words as she sipped the coffee. It was strong and bitter, but Jenny tried to enjoy it anyways. It wasn't like the cups of tea she normally enjoyed every day but thought that she could grow to love it the more she tried it. Perhaps with a bit of sugar and milk it wouldn't be all that bad.

"Let's just keep our wits about us and try our best," Jenny said with a smile. With their coffee gone, they set to work at trying many new things. Once the wash tub had been discovered in the back of the pantry, Margret did her best to explain the process to Jenny. It had been a long time since she'd read anything about washing laundry, and though she had inspected clothes from the maids every time they brought the wash in, Margret had to remember how the washing was done in the first place.

Jenny collected all their laundry and took it outside to scrub and hang up on a clothes' line she found on the side of the house. She tried to follow her mother's instructions perfectly but found that it took a lot of trial and error until she could learn how to make the suds and which way to run the clothes down the scrub board.

Margret was proud of her daughter as she watched her figure out how to use the scrub board. She knew that it wouldn't be easy work, but she was at least happy to see her daughter trying. Margret knew that Jenny had sacrificed a life of ease by denying marrying just any wealthy gentleman. She knew that her daughter had more pride in herself and had a sense of what she wanted in life to simply settle. After watching her daughter for a moment, her heart filled with pride to have raised such a good-natured daughter, Margret then returned inside to try her hand at baking bread and tidying up the house.

As Jenny sat doing the laundry, she tried to take her mother's advice and not think too much about their life in Richmond. She was certainly glad that they'd escaped the horrible memories and whatever distasteful things her uncle had planned for them. Jenny looked around the yard, seeing the mountains rise up in the near distance. They were covered with a thick forest even though Jenny could see the peak of the mountain. Her eyes were drawn to the chickens as they clucked and moved around their pen. She found them to be interesting creatures and watched them for a bit as she scrubbed the laundry the best she could.

Towards the shade of a few trees that were gathered together behind the house, Jenny looked upon a modest sized garden. Most of what had grown seemed to have been harvested already, but as she remembered the pristine gardens that adorned the outside of her family's manner in Richmond, she wondered that if one day she could plant some flowers in the garden as well. Certainly, flowers wouldn't be an important resource in Bear Creek, but she thought it would add a nice touch to the scenery. She could enjoy not only trying her luck at gardening, but also bringing in fresh flowers from the garden, adorning them on the dining table.

As Jenny took in everything around her, she thought of all the possibilities instead of comparing everything to her life in Richmond. She had to keep reminding herself that her childhood life was in the past and what she had for her future was dependent on what she'd be able to create for herself. Jenny understood that she wasn't alone and had her mother for support, but it would take a lot of work. Not only to survive, but perhaps to also show Mathew that she was worthy as any other women in the West as a suitable wife.

CHAPTER 9

Mathew was eager to return home as the sun made its way through the sky and eventually started its descent. It had been a long day, but at least the morning chill had ebbed as the sun warmed the earth once more. Mathew could see that the herd was faring the weather without issue, and it even seemed to rowdy Bailey up. Mathew put his cattle dog through his paces, keeping him lean and sharp. They worked hard together, keeping the cattle healthy by exercising them and making sure they were safe from any predator. Mathew hadn't seen a bear on his property for a long time, but the area wasn't called Bear Creek for nothing. Mathew knew that bears roamed this part of the country openly and that from time to time he'd have to ward off a bear from trying to poach one of his cattle.

Heading back towards the barn to settle in Daniel for the evening, Mathew called Bailey after him and together they headed in from the pasture. They raced to the barn, the thundering of Daniel's hooves sounding on the ground. The wind whipped through Mathew's hair, giving him a sense of flying as they moved quickly across the pasture.

He couldn't help but chuckle as they entered the barn and Mathew was forced to slow Daniel to a walk.

"It seems you win again, Bailey," Mathew said to the collie as he dismounted and led Daniel to his stall. Bailey barked happily as he did several spins before settling down on his haunches. "Best to get that energy out of you now before we go up to the house."

After taking off Daniel's saddle and brushing the draft horse, Mathew filled his feed bag and bid the horse goodnight. Then, Mathew finally made his way to the ranch house with much anticipation flowing over him. He couldn't wait to see what the Phillips women had been up to that day since they were both inexperienced with living in the West. Mathew reasoned that at one point they'd been wealthy enough to hire servants to do all the work for them. He smiled, trying to imagine how well the women were able to do things for themselves today.

Stepping into the house, Mathew was happily surprised to see that the fire had been tended to throughout the day to ensure that the house stayed warm. He smiled as he took off his boots at the door. Bailey barked once as though to announce their return to the house. He padded into the house, sniffing the ground as he went. As Mathew looked down, he realized that the wooden floorboards had been washed and now shone in the light of the setting sun. Several candles burned around the central room, filling the space with plenty of light.

"Oh, good afternoon, Mathew," Jenny said as she came down the hallway, wiping her hands on an apron that she wore over her burgundy day dress. She smiled happily at him before bending down and petting Bailey.

"Seems you two have been busy," Mathew said as he looked all around the room. He sniffed the air, smelling fresh baked bread and seeing several different sized loaves on the table. He chuckled as he approached to get a better look at them.

"Mother's attempt at baking for the first time. Some of them are quite dense, but she reasoned she could make a bread pudding with eggs and milk," Jenny explained.

"They look well enough," Mathew assured her. "I'm not a picky eater at all."

"That is good to know. I've tried my hand at a roast with potatoes and carrots. I look forward to learning your opinion at dinner," Jenny said as she went over to the oven. Mathew watched as she carefully removed the pot roast from the small oven with several hand towels and the use of her apron to protect her hands. As soon as she lifted the lid, the savory aromas of cooked meat filled the air.

"It smells amazing, so I'm sure it will be delicious as well," Mathew said as he started to set the table for dinner. Jenny smiled happily as she put the lid back to let the meat rest. Margret came in through the back door then carrying more buckets of well water.

"Ah, good afternoon, Mr. Jenkins. It's good to see you," Margret said as she set the buckets down by the back door. She took a deep breath, having worked hard all day. She much looked forward to resting this evening.

"Hello, Mrs. Phillips. You're looking in high spirits, I see," Mathew said with a smile.

"Well, I have much to be proud of," Margret said as she filled her cup with water and settled down at the table. "I have baked bread with various degrees of success. The floors have been washed and the main room has been dusted."

"That is quite an accomplishment for sure," Mathew agreed. "I have not done that task in some time, as I'm sure you could tell."

"Well, when you live on your own, I can only imagine you don't have enough hours in the day to get everything done," Margret reasoned before taking a long drink of her water.

Mathew only nodded as he helped finish setting the table. Then, he brought the roast pot to the table with the use of several kitchen towels. Jenny thanked him as she settled at the table herself.

"It was an adventure for sure today," Jenny said as Mathew removed the lid of the roast pan and began to help dish out portions to the women. "I washed all our clothes and dried them on the clothes line. Then I started working on this dinner."

"Ah, yes. Washing clothes can become quite tedious," Mathew said as he settled into his chair. The roast seemed to be cooked perfectly as it had been easy to carve and serve. Everything looked well-seasoned and he was eager to try some of it.

"That is what I soon learned after starting the experiment," Jenny said with a chuckle. "But when I added hot water that I had heated on the stove to the tub, it was much easier to wash the soapy clothes."

Mathew couldn't help but laugh as he sliced one of the loaves of bread. He imagined what it must have looked like for Jenny to struggle with rinsing the clothes of the soap if she'd used too much.

"And to see you both smiling still seems to be a miracle in and of itself," Mathew said. "You've both done such a wonderful job that it would be hard to call you city girls any longer."

Margret chuckled at the thought. "It will take some time to figure everything out," she said. "But I think our first day at the job proved to show us that we are capable of doing more than we ever thought possible."

"Good choice of words, Mother," Jenny agreed. After Mathew said a quick prayer for the food, they began to eat the lovely dinner that Jenny had prepared. She was eager to hear everyone's thoughts since she'd worked hard to follow the recipe in great detail. There were a few spices Jenny hadn't been able to find in the pantry, but as she ate, she thought that it tasted well enough.

"If I hadn't known you'd never cooked a roast before, I would not have believed that this was your first attempt," Mathew said with a happy sigh. "It's cooked perfectly, and the vegetables aren't mush at all." Jenny beamed with pride to hear Mathew's remarks on her food. She couldn't believe him and turned to her mother.

"He's correct, my dear. It is lovely," Margret agreed. The roasted meat seemed to melt in her mouth and she wondered if Cook would have been able to do better.

"Well, it seems I might have an aptitude for cooking then," Jenny said happily as she continued eating as well.

"And the bread is very good, Mrs. Phillips," Mathew added. The older woman chuckled, raising her hand to hide her smile.

"You're too kind, Mr. Jenkins," she replied.

As they ate, an idea came to mind on how these women could become even more self-sufficient. "I understand that both of you are looking for some sort of employment," Mathew said. "Since you both have very cheerful attitudes towards housework, it wouldn't be hard to imagine that both of you could find employment in town doing similar work for the business owners."

Jenny brightened at the idea as she looked towards her mother. "I'm sure we could become proficient enough to offer our services to others," Margret agreed. "We'd have to find our way to town on our own, though."

"I plan to head to town in a day or two for more supplies," Mathew said. "I can teach you both to drive the wagon, and I'm sure my mare would love the exercise. Buttercup doesn't get out that often and she would be great for beginners." Jenny was excited about the idea, remembering Mathew mentioning the idea the night before. But as she looked to her mother, she saw concern in her eyes.

"I think it would be important for us to learn how to drive the wagon into town on our own. Especially if we'll be able to find some work in town," Jenny said. "And of course, we'd make sure to maintain things here as well."

"I'm not too worried about it," Mathew said, sometimes forgetting that he had an arrangement with Jenny. He was simply enjoying her presence in his home and hearing all about their day made him truly smile. Mundane things seemed to bring so much happiness to these women. He was certain that if they learned to hitch Buttercup on their own to the wagon, that nothing would be able to stop them from achieving whatever goal they put into place.

"I will do my best to be a good learner, Mr. Jenkins," Margret said a little doubtfully at the thought of driving a wagon herself. "I find house chores easy enough because I managed my own home for many years and can remember how the servants did things. But I've never watched a horse be hitched up to a wagon before."

"I will admit that hitching up the horse is the hardest part," Mathew said. "But from there, the horse seems to know the rest. I'm sure if I let Daniel, he'd find his way to town and back home with little direction from me." Margret appreciated his reassuring words, but the idea still concerned her. Figuring that was a matter for tomorrow, she rose from the table and bid them good evening.

Jenny watched her mother disappear down the hallway. They'd left the doors open to allow the warm air to heat the rooms, but she worried that her mother would become cold during the night if it became chilly once more. But then Jenny reminded herself that her mother had been a very resilient woman during their travels. She knew that her mother would say something if she became too cold. Therefore, Jenny turned her mind to clearing the table and preserving the loaves of bread her mother had made.

"I'll take care of the leftovers," Mathew said as he also rose to help out. "Bailey usually eats whatever I don't. And the chickens don't mind it, either."

"I'll have to remember that one," Jenny said as she used cloths to wrap the bread and put them in the pantry so they wouldn't dry out too quickly. "I simply don't want anything to go to waste or spoil too quickly."

"That's smart thinking. With winter fast approaching, we'll have to be mindful of several things from staying warm to making sure we don't go through all the supplies too quickly," Mathew explained as he scraped the leftover roast into Bailey's bowl on the floor. The rest Mathew put into a bucket to take out to the chickens in the morning.

Jenny chuckled as she thought about her mother's experiment with bread making. "Then I shall speak to Mother about that before she uses up all your flour," Jenny said.

"That would be wise," Mathew agreed. "I don't want to say anything that might deter either one of you from trying something new when so much must be new for you both."

"But please don't be afraid to speak up," Jenny said as she began to warm some water on the stove to wash the dishes. "We must learn to be as self-reliant as possible. It will be good for us to learn how to do things the right way the first time." Mathew nodded as he came to join Jenny at the sink as he once again took up the job of drying the dishes.

"There are so many single men in town that I'm certain it wouldn't be hard for you to marry one day," Mathew said. "You have many wonderful qualities that any man would find worthy." Jenny smiled, liking to think his words were a form of a compliment instead of a way to motivate her moving on from his ranch.

"At this time, Mathew, I only want to focus on taking care of myself and my mother," Jenny said simply as she began to wash the dishes. "But I am glad to think that you consider me to have many amiable qualities for a city girl." They chuckled together at her words, and Mathew almost said all the things he thought lovely about her. He didn't think now would be the right time as he helped with the dishes. Afterwards, when the kitchen was all cleaned up and Jenny assumed that it would be a good time to retire for the night, Mathew surprised her once again by his kindness.

"Would you care to join me on the front porch? It's a lovely night for seeing the stars and a blanket would keep you warm," Mathew offered as he picked up an afghan from the back of a chair near the fire. Jenny thought about the idea for a moment and then nodded. It would be nice to see the stars.

Jenny took the blanket from Mathew and wrapped it around her shoulders as he pulled his boots back on. He whistled to Bailey, signaling for the dog to follow as they made their way onto the front porch. Mathew gestured to the rocker and Jenny gladly sat down as he took up a position on the front steps. From there, Jenny was able to lean back into the rocker and look up at the stars as they twinkled from high above. The sky was so large and wide, and so bright that Jenny thought she could simply reach up her hand and pluck a star from the sky.

"It's chilly, but absolutely beautiful," Jenny said as she stared up at the stars. Mathew had meant to enjoy the view as well since there wasn't a cloud in the sky, but he couldn't help but watch Jenny instead. Even in the dim light of the night, he could make out her lovely features.

"Yes, beautiful," Mathew said absentmindedly. Bailey rested beside him, laying his head in Mathew's lap as he petted the collie's long fur. For a moment, Mathew could imagine this was his future. He'd spend the evenings with his wife, enjoying the simple things in life. It didn't appear it took much to please Jenny, and she seemed eager to learn all she could to make her own way. These were qualities in a woman that Mathew greatly appreciated. And as he watched her, he wondered if anything would come from their arrangement in the form of romance or love.

Jenny was surprised when Bailey left his master's side and climbed up with his paws on her lap as she sat in the rocker. She chuckled as she petted the dog while he did his best to lick her face.

"Bailey, no!" Mathew said as he tried to bring the dog back to him.

"Oh, Mathew, it's quite alright," Jenny assured as Bailey settled down and simply lay beside her. "I've never had a pet before and find Bailey very comforting."

Mathew sighed with relief, fearing that Bailey had overstepped himself. But as Jenny rocked and petted Bailey, he thought how nice it was that a woman would find his dog comforting. Mathew knew that Bailey had been a big comfort to him over the years, and perhaps Bailey now sensed the same need to comfort Jenny.

"I find it so peaceful here," Jenny eventually said after a moment of silence had passed between them. "I know today was a lot of work, but I was able to go about my day without the fear of someone watching me or judging my actions." Mathew nodded, knowing how nice it was to work for himself instead of someone else.

"Out here, I don't have to worry about society speaking ill of me or my business showing up in the gossip section of the newspaper," Jenny continued. "I'm truly free to be whomever I want to be."

"I'm glad to hear that, Jenny, I really am. I want you to be comfortable in Bear Creek, but I also want you to be careful," Mathew said. He knew that Jenny and her mother weren't exactly aware of everything that the West had to offer settlers.

"Do you mean from bandits and other criminals?" Jenny asked. "There are always stories about such things in the papers back East."

Mathew chuckled at the question. "Yes, Jenny, there are criminals that roam the open road. But that isn't the most serious concern," Mathew explained. "The biggest thing I look out for when I'm out in the pasture looking over the cattle are wild animals. You must understand that Bear Creek was named after the large bear population in this area."

"Bears?" Jenny asked. "Does that mean we should go inside?" She quickly looked away from Mathew as she peered into the night. Darkness surrounded the house and she wondered if there was a bear nearby.

"You're fine, Jenny. I promise," Mathew assured her. "Sometimes a bear will come around the property, but mostly they are up in the hills at the main part of the creek."

"Well, that is certainly good to know." Jenny looked back at Mathew. "What else should I know about the area?"

"For the most part, everyone knows everyone. That will take time for both you and your mother, but once you know who's local, you then can be aware of strangers," Mathew explained.

"My mother will certainly enjoy getting to know everyone. She's always been very social," Jenny said with a smile. "I think that is one of the things that she misses from her old life. Women her age to spend time with."

"Well, both Mrs. Tibet and Mrs. Fry would no doubt make good companions for your mother. And I'll also have to introduce you to Brown Bear. He's the chief of the Sioux Indian tribe that lives up in the hills."

Jenny gasped at the idea of meeting a real Indian. She was nervous about the idea because of all the terrifying reports she'd read in the newspaper. "I had no idea that Indians lived so close to Bear Creek. And you are friends with some of them?" Jenny's eyes went wide at the thought of seeing Indians. Jenny's naivety was really starting to tickle Mathew's funny bone. He did his best to keep from laughing at her in hopes of not making her feel silly for asking the questions.

"Yes, Jenny. I'm good friends with Brown Bear. He and his people are very friendly and peaceful."

"My goodness, real Indians." Jenny looked up at the stars and leaned back in the rocker. "I never thought I'd get to meet an Indian." Mathew couldn't contain his mirth then as he chuckled, doing his best to remain as quiet as possible.

"What is so funny, Mr. Jenkins?" Jenny asked with a smile. She had a good idea but wanted to hear Mathew say it himself.

"Forgive me, Jenny. I find your perspective very refreshing," Mathew said with tact. "I know that Brown Bear will find you equally as amazing."

Jenny sighed and stood. "I always try to impress those I meet." She then made her way towards the front door.

"You've definitely impressed me, Jenny," Mathew said before she could disappear inside. Jenny stopped and looked at him, their eyes locking. She was thankful for the night's darkness because surely Mathew wouldn't be able to see her blush. She simply nodded before hurrying inside. She even forgot to put the blanket back as she went straight to her room and laid it out on her bed before getting ready to sleep. She was finding Mathew even more alluring and thought a good night's rest would settle her nerves and help her to focus on her true intent.

As Mathew had watched Jenny hurrying into the house, he knew that his words had affected her. He had meant to encourage Jenny that he meant no malice with his words, but a part of him wanted her to know that his interest in her was growing. As Mathew returned to petting Bailey, he looked up at the stars and took a deep breath of the chilly night air. He knew things would continue to become interesting around the ranch as the Phillips women continued to experiment and learn new things for themselves. Mathew only hoped that Jenny would come to enjoy living in Bear Creek and not just think of all of this as a way to escape. He wanted to show her that being in the West was a great way to live as well.

# CHAPTER 10

*L*ife seemed to settle into an easy routine for Jenny and Margret as they became more accustomed to living on the ranch with Mathew. For the most part, the women were left to their own devices as Mathew left the house early every morning to tend to the cattle. Therefore, Jenny and Margret felt no pressure in doing the things they could around the house and testing out different recipes from their cookbook. Mathew always found it exciting to return to the house to see what the ladies had accomplished that day. They often laughed about their many pitfalls as they learned to do things on their own. The meals weren't always that great, but it was enough for Mathew. He was just pleased to think they were getting along well enough without the things they normally had in Richmond.

"Well, I must say," Mathew said one evening. "I've never seen the house this clean. Even when Ma was still alive, she was never able to keep on top of the housework like you two are able to."

"Just took some time to figure out how things are done in the West," Margret said. "I was worried that life would be too hard here in Bear Creek compared to Richmond. But I can attest that I like it much more here. It's so peaceful and everything I need I can get myself." Jenny was pleased beyond belief to hear her mother say these words. She was doing her best to get accustomed to things as well and was at least relieved to hear her mother was faring well with all the big changes.

"How about we go into town tomorrow then?" Mathew suggested. "Bailey knows how to watch over the cattle, and we can leave early in the morning."

"I think that's a lovely idea. It will give us an opportunity to meet some locals and perhaps inquire of any cleaning positions," Jenny said, excited about the idea of not only getting to know more people in the area, but perhaps earning some extra money that would go towards finding a place of their own. She dearly missed socializing with friends and attending different gatherings. Jenny hoped that she'd be able to continue doing so in Bear Creek.

"And I suppose it's time that we learned how to drive the wagon," Margret said with a sigh.

"Don't worry, Mother. I'll drive us until you feel more comfortable," Jenny reassured her. Jenny wasn't sure she could learn to do so but understood that she must in order to be an independent woman in the West.

The next morning the three of them left the ranch house together after a light breakfast. Jenny and Margret followed Mathew to the barn where they were introduced to Buttercup, the mare. Jenny and Margret got to see for themselves everything that was in the barn, from the towering stacks of hay that the herd needed in the winter, to the different types of equipment the horses needed to be saddled or pull the wagon. Jenny noted how there were several empty stalls and wondered if these were the only two horses that Mathew had.

"Now, she's an older girl but still full of plenty of spirit," Mathew said as he led the mare from her stall to the center of the barn. Anyone could tell that Buttercup was an older horse, but her eyes twinkled with delight to be going on an adventure. "Her harness is usually hanging on her stall door, so all you have to do is slide it over her and connect it to the pulley on the wagon."

As Mathew showed them how to ready Buttercup, Jenny and Margret paid very close attention. He even had them practice taking off and putting back on Buttercup's harness so they could feel comfortable with the process, and also being around a horse. Jenny and Margret were both nervous at first but found that they could accomplish the task with a little practice. Jenny knew that she needed to remain strong for her mother and tried to hide her nervousness from the horse.

"It's like she doesn't even mind it," Jenny said as she ran her fingers along Buttercup's neck.

"She's been trained for many years to pull a wagon," Mathew stated. "She's used to this by now and should never give you two any trouble."

"I have to say that it isn't as hard as I thought," Margret said as she tried petting the mare, allowing her anxiety to fall away. She found the horsehair very interesting as she ran her fingers over the mane. After they were ready to go, Mathew helped the ladies up into the wagon, and with their cloaks wrapped tightly around them, Mathew urged Buttercup forward and out of the barn.

"Now, leading Buttercup is pretty easy," Mathew said as the mare headed up the drive at a decent pace. "Simply pull this left rein to make her go left, and the right one to go right." Mathew demonstrated as Buttercup moved in the direction she was being guided.

"To have her slow down, you just pull back on the reins to slow her pace," Mathew said. "And when you give the reins some slack, she'll take that as a hint to pick up her pace."

"And what about a whip, Mathew?" Jenny asked. She remembered her uncle's driver always carrying a whip with him to encourage the horses forward.

"If the horses trust you, you won't need a whip to control them," Mathew said, a hard expression crossing his features. "You only need a whip if you have a disobedient horse that is new to you, or you're simply not a good person and the horses can sense that."

Jenny thought about his words, suddenly feeling very sorrowful for her uncle's horses. But instead of focusing on that, Jenny looked at the road ahead. It was still early in the morning and she was looking forward to meeting as many people as possible in town today. She was thinking that they needed to reach town as quickly as possible. She was therefore surprised when Mathew placed the reins in her gloved hands.

"Are you sure about this?" Jenny asked as she gripped the reins, fear running through her suddenly.

"Absolutely," Mathew said with a smile. "Just don't grip them so hard. Relax your hands and arms." Jenny did as instructed and soon found that Buttercup was merely doing all the work.

"It's like she knows the way already," Jenny exclaimed happily.

"She sure does."

Margret smiled at the two as she watched how attentive Mr. Jenkins was to Jenny. "You're a good teacher, Mr. Jenkins," Margret commented with a smile.

"Thank you, Mrs. Phillips. I'm sure my schoolteacher would appreciate to hear so," Mathew said with a chuckle.

"Can you believe it, Mother? I'm driving a wagon," Jenny said happily. Margret laughed at her daughter's excitement. Margret thought that it was good that Jenny was enjoying learning this new task since she wasn't particularly fond of the idea. And after all the devastation they'd been through, she wanted to see her daughter as happy as possible. Margret was starting to think that Mathew would be a good match for Jenny.

"I see, Jenny. You're doing a grand job, and thankfully so since I enjoy being a passenger." The three laughed at the comment as they made their way into town. Mathew talked about all the business owners and people they were bound to meet. Jenny was starting to think that Bear Creek was much larger than she had first reasoned. With so many businesses and local families, the population seemed to be about one hundred and fifty strong. With every passing moment, Jenny looked forward to their arrival in town and making new friends.

MATHEW WAS SITTING on the steps of the church as he waited for Jenny and Margret. After parking the wagon in front of Frys, they'd gone off to make their introductions to the various business owners. At first, Mathew had accompanied them. But after a while, he saw how social the ladies were on their own and decided to take care of a few errands. Now, he waited at the church with the light lunch they'd prepared that morning.

Mathew reflected on the last week as he'd grown accustomed to having the Phillips women in his home. He could tell that he'd been much happier with other people to talk to on a daily basis. He hadn't realized just how lonely he'd become until he had someone to look forward to speaking to every evening. Both Jenny and Margret were good company, but he was very interested in getting to know Jenny better. After all, she was the first young lady he'd been interested in for a long time. And with no other letters having arrived in response to his ad, he was certain that Jenny was more than likely his one shot at finding a decent woman to be his wife.

As he thought of Jenny, he knew that she was much more than just decent. She was not only beautiful, but also strong natured and determined. The fierceness that Mathew had seen in her eyes in the photo she'd sent him could be easily seen in her future as she talked about all her daily accomplishments around the ranch. Both she and Margret seemed to be proud of all that they were able to do each day, and though the tasks were very normal to Mathew, he could tell that it brought a sense of purpose for the women.

Mathew could understand their perspective because he was very proud of his way of managing the ranch all on his own. Though he had to give credit to his well-trained cattle dog, he knew that his daily motivation to do a good job is what allowed him to have a successful ranch. Though, he hoped that one day he could grow his herd and even hire a few cattle hands to help him drive the cattle to auction each year. But for now, Mathew was content on doing the work all on his own.

The only thing that caused Mathew to worry is how sometimes Jenny and Margret compared things to how they used to live in Richmond. He was certain they were only making an honest comparison, but would Jenny truly come to enjoy living in Bear Creek. If they did marry, would she one day regret the decision of moving away from an easy life? Mathew understood that life wasn't perfect in Richmond, but would Jenny ever one day think of a possible alternative that would have her returning in a hurry. He did his best not to think this way, but he had to be realistic as Jenny and Margret continued to learn about Bear Creek and its lack of resources.

A smile came to his face as he noticed that Jenny and Margret were coming his way. They crossed the road from Frys, both with eager smiles on their faces. Mathew could only assume that they'd been successful once again in soliciting their cleaning services to others in town.

"Oh, Mathew, you won't believe the good news we have for you," Jenny said as they joined him on the church's steps.

"Knowing how charming both of you can be, it won't be that hard to believe," Mathew said with a chuckle. Margret was pleased with his response as she settled down onto the steps. It was good to know that her daughter's possible suitor had good opinions of them both.

"Well, despite our keen ability to chat with anyone," Jenny said as she looked to her mother with a smile, "we were able to meet with Mr. and Mrs. Tibet. The inn keepers have asked us to come twice a week to help clean rooms. Mother was very persuasive since she's been looking over a household for years. Mrs. Tibet is even willing to teach us a few things about cooking."

"I knew that she would be willing to show you a thing or two. Mrs.

Tibet has always been very helpful," Mathew said, pleased to hear that someone had hired the women.

"When we went into the bank to make our deposit, Mr. Fritz also agreed to have us come clean the bank once a week," Margret said, a smile on her lips.

"Well, well. What a nice surprise," Mathew exclaimed. "And if any man in town could pay a good wage, that would be Mr. Fritz. He's by far the wealthiest man around."

"And we did get to visit with Mr. and Mrs. Fry for a good while," Jenny said with a chuckle. "They can certainly talk your ear off."

Mathew nodded in agreement. "Since Frys is a central point in town, they get to hear the most news of what is going on. They can talk for hours if you let them," Mathew said.

"Well, they've also agreed to have us come once a week to help around the store," Margret added. Mathew whistled then, surprised to hear the news.

"It seems you two are a force to be reckoned with. You convinced three business owners in one day to let you come and work for them even though your domestic skills are still a work in progress," Mathew said happily. Jenny was all smiles as she nodded.

"I don't think many people can deny us," Jenny said to her mother. Mathew silently agreed that there would be little he'd deny Jenny if she'd ask of him.

"Well then, let us eat and head back to the ranch. I want to make sure we have something decent ready for dinner," Margret said as she started to pass around the sandwiches they'd made that morning. They ate in silence as they looked around the town. It was chilly, but they felt comfortable enough as they enjoyed the meal and each other's company.

"And don't worry, Mathew. We'll still make sure to have the house tidy and dinner on the table every evening," Jenny reassured as Mathew collected Buttercup from the livery stable and hitched her back to the wagon once they'd finished eating.

"I am not too concerned about that, Jenny. I'm just glad to know that you and your mother have found employment for the time being," Mathew replied as he helped the women up into the wagon. As he climbed up himself, he gave Jenny the reins. She excitedly had Buttercup start off at an easy pace as she maneuvered the wagon around to head back out of town.

Mathew was certainly happy for the Phillips women as they chatted about everyone they had met and how they looked forward to working in town. It gave him comfort to know that he'd done a good thing for someone else and knowing that he'd still be able to see Jenny every evening was a nice thought. He couldn't help but think that his admiration for Jenny was growing with every passing day.

"And I heard that there are a few empty apartments in town from Mrs. Fry," Margret said, pulling Mathew from his deep thoughts. The idea of them moving to town did not sit well with him, and that thought surprised him. He knew that a part of their deal was them finding employment so they could get their own accommodation.

"Perhaps we can take a tour of one of them once we find out who owns them," Jenny replied with a kind smile. She wasn't ready to leave the ranch house just yet. She'd just gotten used to being there so that the idea of leaving wasn't that pleasant to think about. Jenny felt comfortable living on the ranch and using the things around the house. She knew how to use the stove and how to keep the fire burning in the chimney to warm the house. And even though the toilet was outside, she found that with the passing days it didn't bother her as much as it had done.

But the more Jenny thought about moving to town now that her and her mother had secured some employment, the more Jenny realized that it wasn't just a familiar place that Jenny was afraid of leaving behind. It was the fact that she had come to truly enjoy Mathew's company. She looked forward to speaking with him every evening over dinner and talking about their day together. He was always so encouraging and seemed genuinely happy to hear about all their success each day as they learned new skills by simply experimenting. Even when they talked about their mistakes, he never made them feel bad or guilty. He laughed with them and tried to teach them new things each day.

As Jenny watched Mathew from out of the corner of her eye from time to time, enjoying how close she sat next to him on the driver's bench, she knew that in her heart she'd started to develop feelings for him. She still wasn't keen on the idea of marriage, and she even reasoned with herself that if she did move into town with her mother that she and Mathew would still be able to see one another. After all, it wasn't that far from town to the ranch. But there was something about living with Mathew that allowed her to see his true character. And when Mathew complimented her on her many good abilities, she could think of many more things about Mathew that she appreciated in a man.

For now, Jenny knew that it would take some time to get into a routine of working and earning an income before they would discuss once more about moving to town. She only hoped that her mother wasn't in a big hurry, and that they'd find their work as enjoyable as they had at the ranch.

## CHAPTER 11

Margret would never have thought that being employed could be so joyful. Though she relied on Jenny to hitch Buttercup up to the wagon and drive them into town almost every morning, Margret found herself enjoying the time she got to spend with the townspeople. While she worked, she learned more about the history of Bear Creek through Mr. and Mrs. Fry, and even more recent events from Mr. Fritz at the bank. And together with Jenny, they were always able to impress the people who'd hired them and fulfill all the duties they'd been given. Margret's years of experience overseeing a household had certainly paid off as she classically trained Jenny in the work she'd learned to do years ago through her studies.

In the afternoons, Jenny and Margret would head back to the ranch after gathering their pay and any supplies they thought they would need at the house. They'd bought a few of the spices that Mathew didn't have in order to create some wonderful dishes and always made sure to have a decent supply of active yeast to make fresh bread in the morning. Margret enjoyed baking all manner of breads and pies, while Jenny was more skilled at the main dishes. Together, they really started to impress Mathew.

"Seems like those cooking lessons with Mrs. Tibet are really starting to pay off, Mrs. Phillips," Mathew said one evening as he sampled her berry pie. Though Margret had made it using canned preserves she'd picked up at the dry goods store, she still thought it had turned out well.

"Why thank you, Mr. Jenkins," Margret replied. "Though I don't think I'd be able to beat Mrs. Tibet's peach cobbler, I do believe I could give her a run for her money." They laughed over the comment as they enjoyed the dessert. Margret and Mrs. Tibet had become rather close over the past few weeks as they found more and more interests they had in common. Mrs. Tibet would not only teach Margret about cooking, but she was happy to talk to a woman of her age about her children and grandchildren that lived a few towns away. It was the type of conversation Margret enjoyed and she could easily see herself spending several days a week in the company of Mrs. Tibet

Jenny was certain that her mother had recovered fully from her grief. She'd watched her become much more like her former self as she visited with everyone she could while they worked in town. Jenny was happy that she didn't find any of the chores exhausting or tedious, and Jenny was happy enough to take on some of the harder jobs just to see her mother enjoying herself again. It was good for her mother to be making friends and Jenny thought that the two older couples really helped brighten her mother's mood.

As Jenny had accompanied her mother each day into town, she too had started to meet the locals. There were several men that she'd met while working in town, to include Mitchel Franks the barber and Sheriff Benning with his deputy, Tanner Williams. Jenny learned quickly that Mathew hadn't been exaggerating when he said that there were many single men in town. And many seemed to be quite eager to make her acquaintance. Although Jenny was kind to everyone she met, she didn't accept any personal invitations to attend dinner at the inn. Secretly, she was hoping to spend alone time with a certain individual that had been on her mind for quite some time.

"Jenny," Mathew said that evening after dinner. "Since you and Mrs. Phillips don't have work in town tomorrow, would you care to join me while I go visit the Sioux Indian camp?" Jenny was quickly pulled from her thoughts as she looked at Mathew. She remembered then about the local Indian tribe and was curious to meet a real Indian.

"I think that would be an interesting experience. I've been eager to meet the Indians ever since you spoke about them the other night," Jenny said. "What do you think, Mother?"

Margret looked between the two young people. This was the first time Mathew had invited Jenny out of the house to do anything together. She knew she could trust Mathew to be a respectful person because he'd shown no signs of foul play since they'd been staying in the ranch house. It had almost been three weeks since they'd come to Bear Creek and Mathew had been nothing but hospitable and respectful to her and Jenny. Margret had a lot of respect for the young man in return.

"Though I do trust you, Mr. Jenkins, it is these Indians that I'm not sure about," Margret said. "I have heard from Mr. Fritz that there is some current situation between them and the miners."

Mathew nodded, knowing that honesty was going to be the best option in this situation. "It is no wonder that you heard such things, Mrs. Phillips. Louis is working hard at helping the Sheriff in this matter," Mathew explained. "And there has been some tension between the two groups in the past. The miners want to search for gold in the area that the Indians live on. Their greed often motivates them to impose on Brown Bear and his people."

"So, you see, Mr. Jenkins, I worry about Jenny's safety while visiting with these Indians. I'm not familiar with their way of life, and the Eastern papers are often filled with horror stories," Margret admitted.

"It is true, Mathew. It's not often that a good thing has ever been written about an Indian," Jenny said. Though she was curious to meet Mathew's friends, she was worried about being safe around Indians.

Mathew thought about his words for a moment. He knew that Margret and Jenny had both brought up valid points. There was still the issue between the Indians and miners, though it seemed to have become a quiet situation for now. And he was well familiar with how White people often treated Indians.

"Mrs. Phillips, I wouldn't suggest this outing with Jenny if I didn't feel that she would be absolutely safe. I've been traveling to the Indian camp for many years now and would trust them with my own life," Mathew said. There was so much conviction in his words that Margret couldn't find any other reason to deny him permission.

"Very well, Mr. Jenkins," Margret said with a hint of a smile on her lips. She was glad that Mathew had finally asked to spend time alone with Jenny. She had high hopes for the young couple and hoped that this outing would allow them both to develop deeper feelings for each other. She quite liked the idea of Mathew becoming her son-in-law.

Jenny was thrilled that her mother had given Mathew permission to take her to the camp. She was filled with mixed emotions over meeting the Indians, but she very much liked the idea of getting to spend some alone time with Mathew. She didn't fear him trying to take advantage of her or try to take away her virtue. But she was very curious to know if she had a romantic attraction to him and if he returned her feelings.

THE FOLLOWING EARLY AFTERNOON, after Mathew had finished looking over the herd and Jenny and Margret had completed all the morning tasks, Mathew came back to the ranch house to collect Jenny and take her to the Indian camp. Jenny said farewell to her mother and stepped out onto the front porch with Mathew.

When she only saw the draft horse out front, Jenny asked, "Won't we be taking the wagon?"

"The wagon won't be able to fit through the trees along the trail. We'll have to ride double on Daniel through the forest," Mathew explained. "I'll help you on first."

Jenny was surprised to learn that she'd be riding double with Mathew. At first, she wondered if Daniel would be able to hold their weight, but as Mathew helped her up onto the saddle, she could feel the strength of the horse below her. Then, Mathew pulled himself up onto the saddle and the horse seemed to bear them with little effort.

"Just keep your arms around my middle here and you shouldn't have to worry about a thing," Mathew instructed. Jenny did as he asked, blushing deeply at wrapping her arms around him. She enjoyed how warm he felt and didn't have to worry about becoming chilled as they traveled. The days had slowly begun to become cooler, but as Jenny held onto Mathew, she was filled with plenty of warmth to ward off the chill of the afternoon.

Together, they rode in silence as Mathew led Daniel away from the ranch and into the surrounding hills and forest. To Jenny, it was like entering a whole other world as they passed through the tree line and seemed to disappear. Like Mathew had said, the trail was narrow and wound through all the large oak trees and up and over ridges. Having never ridden on a horse before, Jenny did her best to relax, to move with the movements of the horse, and not to hold onto Mathew too tightly.

Thoughts of bears spread through Jenny's mind as the sunlight seemed to dim because of the towering trees. She looked all around her, curious to see chipmunks chasing after one another and birds flying by as they swooped below and then up onto the tree branches. She kept her eyes sharp as she took everything in, intent on spotting a bear before it spotted them.

But as they went on, Jenny became more relaxed and less afraid. She very much liked the forest, and as they passed through a creek, she thought the water flowing by sounded lovely. In the distance, she could hear the clanking of something being hit repeatedly and she tried to crane her head to get a better look at the source of the noise. It didn't sound like any natural sound and she wondered if they were nearing the Indian camp.

"Where do you think that sound is coming from?" Jenny was finally forced to break their comfortable silence.

Mathew had been enjoying the way Jenny held onto him. At first it had been very tight, and Mathew knew that Jenny must have been nervous about traveling on horseback for the first time. But he didn't mind the physical touch at all. A part of him thought that he could have spent the entire rest of the day simply roaming around the forest with Jenny, taking in all the views of nature and feeling her so close to him.

"It sounds like the miners," Mathew explained. "The main part of the mine is at the top of these hills where the water flows down from the mountain and forms this creek. A part of this creek then flows alongside my property which I draw the herd's water from." Jenny reasoned that if they were close to the mines, then they were also close to the Indian camp. She did her best to relax because she knew that these Indians were Mathew's friends, and she wanted to make a good impression on them.

The smell of something cooking soon filled the air as the tree line broke again. They came out onto a clearing that seemed to be shielded from sight by the thick trees that surrounded it. If Jenny had been out on her own, she'd never have noticed it despite the pleasant smells. But as soon as Daniel cleared the trees, Jenny saw many things appear before her. Her gaze darted everywhere as she took in the sight of dozens of teepees, Indians walking about in thick deerskin clothing and furs, their long dark hair braided behind them. She was intrigued by the feathers in their hair and the beadwork on their clothes. As a group of children came running by Daniel, shouting their greetings at him, she couldn't help but smile at the sight of their happy faces.

After halting Daniel near the corral, Mathew slid off the horse first, then carefully helped Jenny down. He smiled as he watched her, clearly fascinated by everything around her. As Mathew took off his horse's halter and set him free to run with the Indian ponies, he noticed that Jenny stayed rather close to him even though her eyes seemed to be dancing all about the camp.

"Don't worry," Mathew said as he took her hand in his. "They are very friendly people."

Jenny smiled up at Mathew as she focused on him for a moment. She liked the way he'd taken her hand in his and she squeezed it, feeling reassured that he was staying close to her. She then let him lead her through the camp. As she passed by the Indians, she dipped her head, nodding to them all and smiling. She wanted to show that she was friendly, and some of them mimicked her while others looked at her with the same fascination she showed for them.

Mathew led Jenny to the large fire in the center of the camp. As expected, he found Brown Bear there since the evening meal would soon be finished. Savory aromas filled the air as he moved around the fire and approached the Sioux Chief.

"Hello, Brown Bear," Mathew said in greeting. "May I introduce you to Jenny Phillips." Mathew gestured to Jenny whose eyes had grown large at seeing the Indian Chief. Brown Bear was wearing his chieftain necklace, a substantial piece made with colorful beads and feathers. Mathew smiled at her reaction at seeing the tall Indian, and more so when Brown Bear stood to greet Jenny.

"It is nice to meet you at last, Jenny. Mathew spoke of your awaited arrival with much enthusiasm," Brown Bear said with a chuckle. He was eager to tease Mathew. In return, Mathew scowled at his friend. Jenny smiled as she watched the exchange. She could tell that Brown Bear was a very friendly person.

"I am glad to hear that I was previously spoken of," Jenny said with a smile as she looked at Mathew. He looked a bit sheepish as he nodded.

"Come and sit with my people by the fire. The women will soon be done with their preparations," Brown Bear said as he gestured to a log close to where he and the other elders were sitting. "We shall celebrate your arrival, Jenny."

"Thank you, Brown Bear. That is very kind of you," Jenny said with a genuine smile. Mathew guided her down onto the log which Jenny found to be comfortable enough. She figured that it was more comfortable than sitting on the ground. Jenny watched all around her as the Indian people moved and got ready for the meal. She was intrigued to see how the women pulled pots of clay from the fire coals and removed lids and tanned skin bags to showcase the many dishes they had prepared.

Then, as all the families gathered around, the women worked together to serve the meal and pass out plates and bowls of food. Jenny was surprised by the sheer number that had gathered to eat, and it reminded her of a very large family eating together to celebrate Thanksgiving.

"Do they eat like this every day?" Jenny asked as she passed down the plates of food as they were passed around. Eventually, it was her turn and she graciously accepted a bowl and plate. Jenny didn't recognize the food but could at least say that it all smelled very good.

"The tribe gathers together for almost every meal. Sometimes, families will cook in their teepees when the weather is too cold to gather outside," Mathew explained. "But everyone works together to provide for one another."

"It's like one big family," Jenny marveled.

"Exactly," Mathew agreed. "This is venison stew with a corn bread. In the bowl is blood soup." Jenny's hands trembled as she looked down at the blood soup. She set the bowl down between her feet, not wanting to spill any of it on her and too concerned about how it was made to even try it. Mathew laughed as he saw her do this.

"It's actually very good," Mathew said as he drank the soup from the edge of the bowl. "It doesn't taste like blood."

"You act as though you've tasted blood before," Jenny said with a chuckle. She looked around to see that there were no knives or forks, and that the Indians beside her were just using their fingers. Remembering her mother's words to do as the Romans when in Rome, she mimicked the way they ate and was soon able to taste the delicious stew.

"You know, when you bite the inside of your cheek on accident and taste that almost iron taste?" Mathew explained. He finished the rest of his blood soup then, the dish one of his favorites when he was in camp.

"I suppose so," Jenny said between bites. She was finding the Indian food very delicious, even if she had to use her fingers and bits of corn bread to eat it. When she had finished her plate, she looked down at the blood soup by her feet.

"It is rude to refuse anything given to you by an Indian. I would at least try it and if you honestly don't like it, I'll finish it for you," Mathew said. His eyes were kind and Jenny understood that he wasn't making fun of her. But not wanting to offend any of the Indians, Jenny set her plate aside and picked up the bowl of soup with her hands. Carefully, she raised it to her lips, and closing her eyes, she took a small sip.

Surprised by the earthy flavors that had been combined in an almost creamy texture, Jenny kept her eyes closed as she finished her bowl. It was warm and filled her body with a much-needed heat as the sun continued to fade behind the trees. When she finished, she used her fingers to clean her face and set the empty bowl down on the plate by her feet.

"See, wasn't so bad, was it?" Mathew said with a chuckle as he collected their empty plates and passed them down the line of Indians to be collected at the end of the meal.

"I'm thoroughly surprised that was so good," Jenny agreed. "I can't wait to see the look on Mother's face when I tell her what I had for dinner." Mathew laughed as he nodded.

"That will be a sight to see," he said.

As the meal came to an end, singing and dancing commenced as the maidens rose to move about around the fire. Jenny was mesmerized by their movements and found them enchanting to watch. Some drummed to their song while others whistled. One Indian even played a flute, the combination filling the air with such magical music. Jenny couldn't understand the words but thought she'd never heard such beautiful music in all her life. It was as though the song itself was alive as almost every member of the tribe lifted their voices together in unison. The air felt almost tangible as Jenny sat close to Mathew, watching the dancers circle again and again around the fire.

"I see why you enjoy coming here," Jenny said into Mathew's ear as she leaned close, hoping he'd hear her over the singing.

"There is a sense of community in camp that I don't feel anywhere else," Mathew said back to her, leaning his head down towards her.

"And everyone has been so kind and friendly," Jenny replied. "It is hard to believe anything that has ever been written about Indians."

"I'm sure there are some truths to the stories, but I feel that most get it wrong," Mathew said. They clapped their hands together to the rhythm of the music, feeling the very beat in their souls. Jenny was thinking the celebration was almost spiritual as she felt a lightness in her body that she'd never felt before. A part of her even thought it would be fun to try her best at dancing with the other maidens. She loved the way the fringes on their long gowns moved with their movements, as though they were flying.

From time to time, Mathew focused his eyes only on Jenny. He loved seeing the excited look on her face as she took in everything around her. The celebration was wonderful, and he wanted to thank Brown Bear afterwards for honoring him and Jenny. He knew that Jenny wouldn't have known that these maidens were dancing for her, welcoming her to this land and people. Her happy face entranced Mathew and he felt a need to always make her happy. It was so strong, and it surprised him that he felt this deeply for her.

The sound of a gunshot was so startling that at first Jenny wondered if she had misheard it. But when the singing suddenly stopped and was replaced with shouts of fear and anger, Jenny knew that something was seriously wrong. All the Indians seemed to scatter from the central fire as children were picked up and carried away by their mothers to hide in their teepees. All manner of knives and long spears were quickly collected by all the men, and Mathew pulled a pistol from his holster on his hip as they stood together. Jenny was so frightened that she didn't know what to do or where to run. Mathew kept an arm around her as they started to slowly move away from the fire.

From the trees came a line of men who rushed forward, their rifles and pistols firing towards everyone in the camp. The smell of gun smoke stung Jenny's nose as Mathew fired back. He urged Jenny to find a pile of wood to hide behind or a teepee to hide in; something that would offer some protection. Out in the open they were likely to be shot. Jenny turned on her heels and picked up her skirts as she dashed away. Thinking Mathew was right behind her, Jenny ducked inside the nearest teepee and startled a group of Indian women who had been hiding together. Jenny sat down with them and placed her hands over her eyes, afraid of the chaos around her.

She listened as men screamed and shouted. She knew that some cries were of pain and that more than likely someone was currently dying in the camp. She couldn't wrap her mind around what was happening and only wished that Mathew would come and save her. She thought he'd been right behind her, but so far he hadn't come through the tent flap. She prayed out loud as she asked the good Lord to protect her. As she listened to the Indian woman chant beside her, she reasoned that they were doing the same thing.

Mathew ducked behind a pile of chopped wood that was positioned close to the central fire that would give him some sort of protection. He then recognized some of the attacking men as miners. He couldn't fathom why they were attacking now or why, and thought perhaps they only planned to scare the camp. But as Mathew saw a few dead Sioux Indians near the fire where they had been caught off guard and shot down, Mathew knew that war had officially begun between the Indians and the miners.

War trills filled the air as the Indians rushed the miners as they tried to reload their rifles and guns. Mathew watched as he waited for the battle to be over. Glancing behind him, he saw that Jenny was no longer with him. He looked around, trying to find any sign of her. Not wanting to move from his position until everything had settled, he looked towards all the teepees and hoped that she'd darted inside of one of them.

Looking back at the battle near the tree line, Mathew waited until there was a clear opening before ducking out from behind the wood pile and firing at the approaching miners. There was a large group of them, and as he aimed and took fire, Mathew was able to take a few of them down before he needed to withdraw the long knife from his boot and continue forward for hand-to-hand fighting. Most of the miners were surprised when Mathew struck at them, giving him the opportunity to distract them before slashing across their chests and defending arms. He moved swiftly with his Indians friends as they fought back the threatening miners.

When the flap of the tent was pulled open, Jenny looked towards it with hope in her eyes. But when two dirty men came in, dread soon filled her as she stood with the other women and joined the concerted push they made to the back of the teepee.

"Alright, ladies. Come with us peacefully and no one gets hurts," one of the men said. He gestured towards the open tent flap with one hand while the other held a gun pointed towards them. Seeming to understand what he wanted, the Indian women started to walk slowly from the teepee in a line, their heads raised high. Jenny wasn't sure what to do since she wasn't an Indian but as the miner focused his pistol on her, she got moving right away and made sure to stay close to the other women.

The moment they were out of the teepee, the sound of the battle raging on filled Jenny's ears. She cringed, hating to hear the screams of people in pain as men on both sides were struck down. Jenny was so distracted by the fighting that when one of the miners tried to bind her hands, she struck out, fearful of losing her own life.

"Hold still, you Injun lover," said the miner as he struck Jenny back, causing her to fall hard to the ground. She looked up at the man as he neared her and she did her best to kick him in the leg as hard as she could to get him to leave her alone. She needed to find Mathew and get out of there. But just as she rose to her feet, she felt a hot pain ripple through her as something sliced deep into her back. She cried out in pain as she collapsed onto the ground, wriggling in an attempt to get away from her attacker.

"That will be enough out of you," came a voice. It was the last thing Jenny heard before her head was struck from behind and she collapsed, unconscious.

The sound of a woman screaming caught the attention of several of the Indian braves, and Mathew. He wanted to look back to the camp to see who'd been hurt or if any of the miners had broken through the Indian line of defense. But as Mathew was faced with two attackers at once, he was unable to go to the aid of the person who was obviously in trouble. With a new sense of determination, Mathew quickly sliced with his long knife at his attackers, drawing blood and showing them that he could take care of his own.

"Retreat!" a man cried in English. The miners stumbled back and disappeared into the trees. It was obvious that they were outnumbered and now they ran for their lives. Knowing the forest like the back of their hands, the Indian braves rushed after them, intent on taking as many lives as possible. The cries of dying men soon filled the forest as the fleeing miners were hunted down and slain.

Mathew was panting hard. He tried his best to recapture his breath and moved slowly back to the central fire where Brown Bear was regrouping with his warriors. Blood smeared most of their clothing and arms, and Mathew knew these Indians were doing what they were trained best to do. The men of this tribe had been taught from a young age to protect the women and children of their tribe, and tonight they'd proven themselves worthy of being called Indian braves.

"Mathew, are you and Jenny alright?" Brown Bear said as he clasped his hands onto Mathew's shoulder. It felt sore, but Mathew didn't give a hint to his injury. As Mathew looked up at Brown Bear, he saw a darkness in his eyes that told Mathew that he'd enjoyed taking the lives of those who had attacked the camp. But Mathew pushed the thought from his mind.

"Jenny and I got separated. I need to go and look for her," Mathew said.

"Go and look. Be quick. We must speak about this matter with Sheriff Benning," Brown Bear said with much concern in his voice. He might have been proud of defending his people, however he knew that there would be consequences for taking the lives of so many.

Mathew nodded to Brown Bear as he left the circle of warriors and went in search of Jenny. Women had started to come out of the teepees with their children and elderly. Mathew's eyes looked through all the many worried faces, the sounds of sadness rising as families began to grieve for their lost loved ones. But no matter how far Mathew searched or the number of times he made his way through the camp, he couldn't find Jenny anywhere.

Hoping that she had made her way back to the central fire, Mathew found his way back there, jogging and moving through the crowd hoping to find Jenny amongst the throng. When he felt a pair of hands on him, Mathew was startled and had to hold back from striking as he turned and looked up into Brown Bear's face. There was much concern in his eyes and his stomach clenched as dreadful thoughts roamed through his mind.

"Mathew, it has been reported that some of the women have been captured and taken hostage. Jenny may be with them," Brown Bear explained with his hands resting heavily on Mathew's shoulders. He felt terrible to tell his friend this news, and almost embarrassed that he and his warriors couldn't protect all his people.

"Where? Where do you think they have taken them?" Mathew asked as he got over his fright.

"I have gathered a search party and Running Stag is leading it. We will leave once we've secured the camp and regrouped," Brown Bear said, speaking slowly to calm Mathew. But a burning rage had been sparked inside of him at the thought of anyone hurting Jenny.

"I want to go with you," Mathew said, determination rippling from his voice.

"Of course, Mathew. You are a good warrior and we can use all the men we can get," Brown Bear said, pleased with Mathew's response. Then together, they started working to gather all the able men to go in search for the women who had been captured and led away from the camp.

# CHAPTER 12

Jenny didn't come to until she felt her back being pressed up against something hard. The slash in her back caused her to scream out in pain, her eyes shooting open as she looked around her with fear. Cords were wrapped around her torso, binding her to a tree with the other Indian maidens. She was tied so tightly against the tree trunk, her back protested the harsh contact.

"What do you want with us?" Jenny demanded to know. Her vision was blurry, but she could make out a fire burning in a pit in front of her. She could smell the stench of sweat and blood, and she felt cold and wet from the blood that seeped from her back. She shivered, wishing she could lie next to the fire.

"The Indians either pack up and leave this place or we're going to start killing off their women," a man said in a dark voice. Jenny looked towards the voice and could make out three men standing together.

"But, Boss. You didn't say anythin' about killin' women," came a startled voice.

"Shut up, Mason. We have to do this in order to find their gold," the ringleader said, slapping Mason in the face to get him to be quiet.

"You can't do this," Jenny said. "These are innocent women."

"None of ya is innocent," the ringleader said as he neared Jenny. "And as soon as we make our demands, you're the first one I'm killin'." The man spit on Jenny. She moved her head to avoid his spittle but the movement caused more pain to fill her body. So much so that she passed out once again.

Now wearing moccasins instead of boots Mathew and the Indian braves moved swiftly and quietly through the forest darting their way through the trees even though it was very dark. With Running Stag at the lead, Mathew did his best to keep his eyes on the man so he wouldn't get lost in the woods by himself.

The sound of a woman screaming stopped them all dead in their tracks. Running Stag pointed towards a direction, and as Mathew looked, he could make out the faint glow of a campfire. They moved together towards the sound and sight of the camp, making sure not to make any noise so as to surprise the men that had kidnapped the women. Mathew's heart beat hard in his chest as he hoped that Jenny was safe.

As they neared the fire they fanned out to surround the camp. Mathew only noticed three men but realized that one of them had fiery red hair. He wondered if that man could be Geoffrey, the Irish foreman who managed all the miners. Regardless, Mathew was looking forward to taking these men down and making sure the women returned safely to their families. Furthermore, Mathew had made a promise to Mrs. Phillips that he'd keep Jenny safe and he intended to be true to his word.

A gesture from Brown Bear sent the group of Indians and Mathew ambushing the camp. Before the miners could even shout in surprise, they were taken down, knives slashing and disarming them before they could fire their pistols.

"Don't kill them," Brown Bear shouted in his language to the Indian braves. He made eye contact with Running Stag, positioned to scalp the man that was flailing about at his feet, pure terror in his eyes. "They must be turned over to the White people for punishment."

"But that is not our way, Brown Bear. These men deserve to die," Running Stag said as he pressed his knife to the top of the man's head, a bead of blood tricking down his forehead.

"Yes, Running Stag, they do deserve it. But let us not bring more White men coming after us because we have already killed so many," Brown Bear reasoned. "They need to tell the White people what they've done and that we simply defended ourselves." Mathew didn't bother watching the pair argue. Already the other two miners had been bound and knocked unconscious. One of the Indian braves had started to cut the ropes which bound the women to a large tree. As he moved to help, that was when he saw Jenny's slumped form.

"Oh God, Jenny!" Mathew cried out as he severed the ropes from around her and pulled her to his chest, holding her tight. But as his arms wound around her, he felt a warm, slick feeling run across his palm. He looked down Jenny's back then to see she was covered in blood.

"Brown Bear! Jenny's hurt bad!" Mathew yelled, attracting the Chief's attention to him.

"Let's get her back to camp, Mathew. White Raven will be able to tend her wounds there," Brown Bear said as he came to Mathew's side and began to inspect the wound on Jenny's back. Mathew lifted Jenny into his arms and Brown Bear led him personally back to camp, relying on his warriors to do the right thing and bring the captured men back to camp as well.

Jenny's weight was a burden, but Mathew ignored the pain in his arms as he moved as fast as he could through the forest to reach the Indian's medicine man. Town was too far to take Jenny and try to wake Dr. Harvey and get him to the clinic to tend to Jenny. He would have to rely on Brown Bear's judgement that their medicine man would be able to save Jenny's life.

As Brown Bear moved swiftly through the forest, leading Mathew by the arm since the man's eyes wouldn't be used to the forest at night the way his were, he sent up several prayers to the Great Spirit. He asked that his dead brothers would be welcomed home to the Great Spirit and that their families would be comforted. He asked for help in dealing with the White people, that no more destruction would come to his people. And furthermore, he prayed that Jenny's life might be saved. After seeing the amount of blood on Jenny, Brown Bear worried that the woman wouldn't live.

As they came jogging back into camp, Brown Bear found a warm place by the central fire for Jenny. As Mathew laid her down, Brown Bear sent word for White Raven to come at once. Though he was certain that many had sustained injuries, Brown Bear had a feeling that many things relied on this White woman being able to recover. The moment that White Raven came running to the central fire, Brown Bear quickly explained the situation.

The man knelt beside Jenny and rolled her over to inspect the wound. He didn't say a word as he looked at the knife mark with much concern. He quickly started asking for different supplies, and Brown Bear sent braves to gather what he needed. Brown Bear watched as Mathew sat on the other side of Jenny, moving her hair out of her face and looking down at her, his expression filled with concern.

White Raven moved fast to remove the White woman's clothes from her back, using his knife to cut away the many layers. Then, he cleansed the skin and the wound with fire water before using a sharp thorn and horsehair to close the wound.

"Mathew," Brown Bear said, forcing Mathew's attention. "You should head to town. Notify Sheriff Benning what has happened."

"And I should go get Dr. Harvey as well," Mathew said as he looked back down at Jenny's pale face one more time before standing. "I won't be long." Brown Bear grunted his approval as Mathew took off through the camp, collecting Daniel from the corral of startled horses. Then, after he mounted the draft horse, Mathew started carefully making his way through the forest and away from the camp. Every instinct told Mathew to push Daniel at a fast trot but he knew he wouldn't be a help to anyone if he went crashing to the ground. Panic swept over him as he thought about the conversations he was about to have with Jacob and Dr. Harvey. And even worse, he dreaded sharing the horrible news with Mrs. Phillips.

"That mother is going to kill me for sure," Mathew said to himself, thinking of the last conversation he'd had with Mrs. Phillips. Even when they'd discussed the tension between the miners and Brown Bear's people, he'd never imagined something like this would happen. Urging his horse a bit faster, Mathew prayed that Jenny would be ok.

When he broke through the tree line at the bottom of the hill, it was like Mathew for the first time could see completely clearly as the moon lit the wide-open spaces before him with its cool silvery light. Urging Daniel into a gallop, Mathew made his way to town, the beat of the horse's hooves seeming to echo all around him. Mathew did his best to keep his wits about him, knowing there was much work to be done tonight still. As he glanced down at his arms, he realized that he had much blood on him and would need to find a place to clean up before he headed back to the ranch to tell Mrs. Phillips the news.

As Mathew made it onto the main town road he headed straight for the Sheriff's Office. There was a small apartment upstairs that Jacob used. It allowed him to be available during any hour of the night in case of an emergency. And considering what had just transpired, Mathew considered this an emergency.

Mathew leapt off of his horse's back the moment they came to a stop. He walked up the front porch and banged on the door loud enough that he'd hopefully wake Jacob. He pounded on the door repeatedly until he could hear Jacob's voice coming down from above.

"I hear ya! Hold your horses!" Jacob yelled. When he did open the door, Mathew saw the man was only wearing his underwear.

"I was in the Indian camp with Jenny when the miners attacked. Many are dead and Jenny needs a doctor," Mathew said so quickly that he didn't have a moment to really think about his words. Jacob stared at him for a good full minute before the importance of what had been said seemed to click in his brain. Without saying a word,

Jacob turned and dashed up the stairs to throw on some clothes. Mathew stepped into the Sheriff's Office and closed the door behind him, waiting patiently for the Sheriff to return.

"You and Jenny both witnessed the miners attacking?" Jacob called down the stairs before he came jogging down them, pulling on the duster and Stetson that hung by the front door.

"Yes, Jacob. After the skirmish, three miners even captured a bunch of Indian women and Jenny. She's hurt real bad, but we were able to rescue them and capture these villians," Mathew explained as he followed Jacob quickly out the front door.

"Alright, Mathew. Go wake Dr. Harvey and meet me back at the camp. I have to get my horse saddled up and then I'll make my way there," Jacob said in parting as he jogged around the building to the livery stables that sat behind the buildings along the main road.

Mathew didn't hesitate as he pulled himself back onto his horse and turned Daniel around to travel a bit out of town to Dr. Harvey's small home. He knew that Jacob could find his own way to the camp, and now he needed the doctor's help to not only treat the wounded, but also save Jenny's life. Pure determination propelled Mathew forward as he sent Daniel out of town at a fast pace. He was grateful for the bright moonlight to guide his way as Daniel thundered over the open plains.

Mathew didn't bother tethering Daniel to the hitching post when he got to the older man's home. He simply slipped out of the saddle and ran up to the front porch where he hammered his fist on the door. Though an elderly man, Dr. Harvey was quick to answer the door, having been summoned all his career in the middle of the night for medical emergencies. Lamp light flooded the front porch as Dr. Harvey opened the door, the lamp leading his way.

"What is it, Mathew?" Dr. Harvey was already dressed for the occasion, and Mathew wondered if the man slept in his clothes just in case he was called out to an emergency in the middle of the night.

"Miners attacked the Indian camp up in the hills. Many are injured, and Jenny Phillips is badly hurt," Mathew quickly explained.

Dr. Harvey nodded as he reached down to just inside the door and picked up his medical bag before stepping out onto the porch and shutting the door.

"I'll get my horse and head there straight away," Dr. Harvey said.

"But do you know the way, sir?" Mathew asked as he followed the doctor off the porch.

"Son, I've been treating people of all races in this land way before you were born," Dr Harvey said with a chuckle. "Don't worry, I know the way to the Indian camp." Mathew was impressed by the man as he went around the house to the small stable. He heard the nicker of his horse and knew that he could trust the doctor.

As Mathew pulled himself back onto his horse, he turned Daniel towards home. He sent the horse into a fast gallop once more, knowing that Daniel would recognize the way home. He needed to reach Mrs. Phillips and bring her to the camp as quickly as he could. If it came to it Mathew didn't want Jenny passing away before her mother had a chance to be with her. Just the idea of Jenny dying was enough to cause Mathew's stomach to tighten. He knew he didn't have time on his side, so he urged the horse faster.

Mathew's body was covered in sweat as he reached his ranch. He feared telling Mrs. Phillips what had happened and that her daughter was not in good health. Before heading into the house, Mathew took a few minutes to saddle Buttercup, knowing that Mrs. Phillips would need a horse to reach camp and that the forest was too dense for a wagon to get through. He hated having to force the woman to ride for the first time, but he knew that she'd want to see her daughter as quickly as she could.

With both Buttercup and Daniel in hand, he led the horses to the front of the house and hitched their reins to the front porch before finally making his way inside. Mathew saw that a few candles still glowed from the dining table. Mrs. Phillips was resting in a chair near the fire, no doubt having wanted to stay up and make sure they'd returned okay. At her feet was Bailey, seeming to want to watch over the older woman. His tail started to wag back and forth, swishing against Mrs. Phillips' dress. Mathew hushed him, causing Bailey to lay still once more.

Guilt wound its way up through Mathew as he slowly went over to the woman. After setting a few more logs on the fire to build it up, not wanting the house to get cold, he then gently nudged Mrs. Phillips' shoulder until she began to wake.

"My goodness," Margret said as she woke and realized she'd fallen asleep by the fire. Then she focused her eyes on Mathew and saw the concern in his face. "Mathew, what has happened?" Fear overcame Margret as all manner of dreadful thoughts raced through her mind.

"Jenny is hurt, Mrs. Phillips," Mathew said slowly, his hand still resting on her shoulder. "The miners attacked the Indian camp and she is there now being treated for her injuries." Mathew felt that it wasn't time yet to share all the details, but for now he'd share enough to show Jenny's mother that she needed to come quickly.

Margret's eyes grew wide as she tossed what Mathew had said through her mind. Slowly, she pushed herself to her feet, setting aside the afghan blanket she'd used to cover herself. She was thankful that she was still dressed with her traveling boots on because she had a great desire to see Jenny for herself.

"Mathew, take me to see my daughter," Margret said as she went to the front door and took her cloak off the front peg and pulled it around her shoulders before pulling on her bonnet to keep her head warm. She couldn't imagine how cold it must be outside now, but she wasn't going to let a little cold keep her from seeing Jenny.

"Best keep the blanket as well," Mathew said as he brought the afghan and wrapped it around Mrs. Phillips before leading her outside into the cold night. "Stay home, Bailey," Mathew called to the dog before pulling the front door closed. He knew that Bailey would only worry about him and it was best to keep him inside where it was warmer.

"Where's the wagon?" Margret asked as she noticed both horses saddled in front of the house.

"Not enough room for it on the trail," Mathew explained as he led

Mrs. Phillips over to Buttercup. "Now put your left foot in the stirrup, hold the saddle horn and lift up with all your might. I'll support you till you can get your other leg up and over the saddle."

"This is very unladylike," Margret said, a bit irritated. But she didn't have time to argue right now. She needed to see Jenny for herself and ensure that she was well. Mathew was just thankful that it was dark as he helped Mrs. Phillips up into the saddle. It was a struggle but Margret finally managed to get into the saddle.

"Now, I'm going to lead Buttercup and hold onto her reins since it's dark and I know the way," Mathew explained as he took the reins before pulling himself back into Daniel's saddle. He knew he'd have to give Daniel a thorough brush down and plenty of treats after tonight. He prayed the horse had enough energy left in him after the ride into town and back to the ranch. He needed his trusty stead to carry him on one more trip back to the camp.

"Just hold on tightly to the saddle, Mrs. Phillips," Mathew said as he urged the horses forward and away from the ranch. He knew he couldn't go as fast as he would have liked since Mrs. Phillips wasn't an experienced rider. And once they crossed the tree line as the trail went up into the hills, the way seemed even darker than before. He was grateful he knew it so well.

Margret was riddled with fear and worry. She wanted to know what had happened to her daughter, what condition she was currently in, and what was being done to help her. Margret was also terrified of riding a horse and even more so when she could barely see in front of her. Riding astride in the saddle was very uncomfortable for Margret and she did her best to move with Buttercup instead of trying to find her own comfortable rhythm. Yet she had to be grateful that Mathew had come for her instead of waiting till the morning.

"Mathew, you need to tell me what happened," Margret said once she was able to overcome her fear of riding a horse just long enough to find her voice again.

"The Indian maidens had been dancing and singing while the tribe played music in celebration of Jenny's arrival to the area," Mathew began to explain. "It was during the celebration that the miners attacked." Mathew paused for a moment as he remembered the first streak of fear that had run through him the moment he realized what was happening. It seemed like a lifetime ago instead of just a few hours.

"They ambushed the camp and fired upon everyone that had gathered for the celebration. Many Indians died immediately, but once everyone realized what was going on, the Indian braves soon began protecting their people," Mathew continued. "The miners were eventually pushed back and they retreated when they realized they were outnumbered.

"During the attack, three miners captured some Indian women, including Jenny. She must have been injured then as she was taken from camp. Once the skirmish was over and it was found out about the capture of the women, Brown Bear organized a search party and we were able to take down the miners and rescue them." Margret fell silent after Mathew had finished talking. She could tell that he was hiding certain details from her, but figured she'd know soon enough the extent of Jenny's injuries.

"White Raven, the Indian's medicine man, was treating Jenny's wounds when I left. I woke Sheriff Benning and Dr. Harvey. They should be at the camp now," Mathew added. His words brought some relief to Margret as she searched the darkness in front of her for some signs of a camp. She was glad that at least someone was seeing to her daughter, and that the authorities had been made privy to the events of tonight. As they traveled through the dark forest, Margret began to silently pray that she'd arrive to this Indian camp and find her daughter at least alive.

# CHAPTER 13

*J*enny's mind seemed to come alive before she realized that she was waking from the deep sleep she'd fallen into. She tried to work out where she was and why she was laying down on something that was rather soft like animal fur. Jenny wiggled her fingers, feeling the soft fur below her. A weight was over her entire body, and she knew she'd been covered by some sort of blanket. She felt warm and safe, and almost considered falling back to sleep. But as the memories of the kidnapping came flooding into her mind, she opened her eyes wide, afraid of where she was.

The walls of a teepee surrounded her as she looked up, the smoke from the fire beside her rising to escape through the small opening at the top. Jenny remembered being in a teepee when she had tried to hide with the other Indian women. She remembered trying to escape their capture and sustaining a nasty knife wound on her back. She tried to move her shoulder now and realized that it was way too painful to do so. So, she remained still as she tried to remember anything else. For a moment, she'd been conscious of being tied to a tree. But how she ended up in a teepee again was beyond her knowledge.

As Jenny slowly turned her head to see what else was in the teepee, she was shocked when her eyes settled on her mother, sleeping peaceful beside her on a similar bed of furs. Her mother lay on her side as she slept peacefully. Jenny didn't understand how her mother had made her way into the camp, but she was certainly grateful to see a familiar face.

Another form lay near the tent flap by her feet. As Jenny's eyes focused on the figure, she realized it was Mathew. His long brown hair had fallen over his face, but she knew it was him. She smiled as she saw him sleeping so peacefully on a mat. His coat was tucked around him and she wondered why he didn't have any furs to keep him warm. Jenny wanted to move and give him some of hers, but her body felt so weak and she was afraid of hurting her wounded shoulder even more that she didn't dare try to move.

Moving her leg slowly, she was able to knock her foot against Mathew. He stirred in his sleep. She had to do it a few times to wake him up, but eventually he turned his head towards her, pushing his hair out of his face before his hazel eyes met her sky blue ones. She smiled at him, finding it a bit humorous to see him in his current condition.

"Are you alright?" Mathew whispered as he pushed himself up off the ground and came to sit cross legged next to her. His eyes moved to Mrs. Phillips and saw that she was still sleeping peacefully. They'd been up all night waiting to see if Jenny would wake, but eventually the older woman had fallen asleep and he'd passed out shortly after. Mathew felt exhausted, but happy to see that Jenny had regained consciousness.

"I'm very stiff and sore," Jenny said, knowing that honesty was the best policy. There was no point telling Mathew a lie when she currently felt so much pain. "My shoulder hurts pretty bad."

Mathew nodded, figuring that much. "White Raven patched you up pretty good, and Dr. Harvey said he couldn't have done a better job. He explained you'd sustained a pretty deep wound," Mathew said.

Jenny sighed as she remembered trying to fight off the men that were capturing her and all the women. "When the miners came into the teepee, I was so afraid. They pointed their guns at us to get us to move. But when they tried to bind my hands, I panicked. I struck back and got stabbed in return," Jenny explained. Pain seemed to wash over Mathew's face. He looked away from her then and she wished she could raise her hand to force his eyes back on hers.

"Mathew, what is it?" she asked when she noticed tears in his eyes. She moved her hand slowly, bringing it out from underneath the blanket of furs till she could wrap her fingers softly around his. He gripped her hand, finding comfort in her touch.

"I just feel so terrible, Jenny," Mathew said as he glanced back down at her. She still looked so pale and frail that he was afraid to hold her hand too tightly. "I promised your mother that I would protect you and now here you are."

Jenny shook her head slowly, the effort causing her head to hurt. But she needed Mathew to understand that none of this was his fault. "You didn't tell those miners to do this to the Indians or me. You have nothing to feel sorry for," Jenny said. "It is no one's fault beside those cruel men's."

Mathew nodded only because he didn't want to argue with Jenny right now. There was still this painful guilty feeling deep inside of him, and he wondered if he'd ever be able to be free of it.

"Brown Bear and his Indian braves and I tracked you and the other women to a small campsite not far from here. That's how we were able to rescue you and the other women," Mathew explained as he tried his best to get control over his emotions. "The miners that captured you and the Indian maidens are in jail. After I made sure you were in good hands, I raced to town to get Sheriff Benning and Dr. Harvey. Then I went to the ranch to lead your mother to camp."

Jenny smiled at him, thinking Mathew was the bravest man she knew. "How on earth did you get my mother here?" Jenny asked in a soft voice.

Mathew smiled as he recalled the memory. "I helped her onto Buttercup and led them both here," he explained.

"My mother rode a horse?" Jenny asked with wide eyes. A bright smile came to her face at the thought of it. Mathew simply nodded, confirming what she'd said. "My goodness, how I'd love to see that." Mathew chuckled lightly as he looked down at the woman he thought he'd lost. He was overcome with such an emotional surge of gratitude that he had to wipe his eyes on his shirt sleeve.

"I'm sure you're hungry. How about I go get you something to eat and drink?" Mathew suggested, needing a moment alone to get a grip on his emotions.

"That would be great. I'm hoping some food and something to drink will take away this headache," Jenny said as she slipped her hand back under the furs while Mathew rose steadily to his feet.

"I'll let White Raven know you're awake so he can tend to your wound," Mathew said before he slipped out of the teepee.

The moment he disappeared, Jenny wished he was back by her side holding her hand. She'd taken such comfort from feeling him close to her that she never wanted to let his hand go. Jenny was surprised by her feelings and the longing she'd developed for Mathew. She reasoned that almost dying would have a strong effect on her state of mind for a long time. She only hoped that as she recovered, her feelings for Mathew would remain. She thought so strongly of him that she was starting to consider the idea of marriage to a man like him. She realized that she wouldn't mind it if Mathew even asked to officially court her.

Jenny sighed as she turned to look at her mother. She hated to have scared her, especially after everything they'd been through together. Jenny had wanted to provide a happy future for them both, but they had learned the hard way that there were still dangers in the West. She couldn't blame the Indians for any of this disaster because they'd all been so kind and helpful to her. Their medicine man had even tended to her wounds, and they'd provided a safe place for her to rest and stay warm. She knew that somehow she'd find a way to thank them, but also to reassure her mother that she would be fine and they would continue to thrive in Bear Creek.

After a time, Mathew returned with a wooden bowl and cup and settled back into his spot next to Jenny. "White Raven says he'll be by shortly to redress your wound. But here is some chicken broth and marshmallow root tea for the pain," Mathew explained. Setting the bowl and cup aside, he then helped Jenny sit up slowly. Jenny felt the pain in her shoulder ripple through her body, but she did her best to keep quiet so that her mother would continue to sleep. She was breathing hard by the time she sat up. Mathew rearranged the blankets around her to keep her warm. Her gown and undergarments had been cut away to expose her back and he didn't want Jenny to feel uncomfortable.

Once settled, Jenny first tried the tea. The taste was pleasant enough, and she was grateful for being able to warm her hands through holding the hot cup. She took slow sips, but it seemed to work well enough by the time she finished drinking it all. Then, she switched the empty cup with Mathew for the full bowl of chicken broth. Again, she took her time as she sipped at the hot liquid, feeling her body seem to come alive as all her pain was soothed.

"Much better," Jenny said with a smile as she handed the bowl back to Mathew. She felt exhausted once more, and with Mathew's help, settled back onto the bed of furs just as an older Indian came into the tent.

"This is White Raven," Mathew explained as he moved out of the way so the medicine man could check on Jenny. She simply smiled at White Raven before following his hand gestures to roll onto her side so he could check her wounds.

As White Raven worked, slowly pulling back the layers of clean cloth he'd used to bandage the wound, he was pleased to see that the bleeding had stopped and that his stitch work had held. He replaced the soiled linens with clean ones as he used a mud mixture to adhere the strips of cloth to the skin. It would also keep the wound from becoming dirty and promote quick healing.

Jenny waited patiently, feeling pain spread out through her as the Indian touched the sensitive skin. But when she felt him apply the mixture, seeming to seal away her wound, she found it very comforting and soothing. So much so that she felt pain begin to fade away. She didn't understand the man's words as the Indian started to chant while he worked. But she was thankful for whatever he was doing because it seemed to work wonders.

Eventually White Raven eased Jenny onto her back once more. He pulled the furs over her and placed his hand to her head as he finished saying his prayer. He then gave both her and Mathew a nod before he stood and left the teepee. He had many people to look after but was pleased to see that the White woman was both awake and healing quickly.

"I guess that means you're going to make it," Mathew said with a chuckle. He knew very little Sioux language and didn't know how to communicate with White Raven. But even though there was a language barrier, he seemed to understand what White Raven was saying. He recognized an Indian prayer and was thankful that the older man did not judge Jenny based on the color of her skin and had agreed to help her anyways.

"I'm glad to hear that," Jenny said as she closed her eyes for a moment. She felt very tired but was enjoying this time with Mathew as well.

"You should probably get some sleep," Mathew said softly. "It is still very early in the morning and the more rest you get the faster you will heal."

"Alright," Jenny said and slipped back into her subconscious. Mathew sat and watched her for some time, wanting to reach out and move back her auburn hair from her face. But with her mother sleeping so close by, he didn't want to do anything that might be frowned upon. He wanted to show Jenny the utmost respect and didn't want to appear to be forward. So instead, he only looked at the young lady that was no doubt capturing his heart.

After a time, Mathew rose and left the teepee. He stretched his arms and legs as sleeping on the ground had made him feel stiff. But he didn't have any time to waste. He needed to get back to the ranch to oversee the cattle and let Bailey out of the house. Yet he also needed to speak with Jacob and see what was happening with the miners in jail.

As Mathew crossed the camp to reach the horse corral to ride home with Daniel and Buttercup, he was swiftly approached by Brown Bear. The Indian Chief looked exhausted and he wondered if the man had gotten any sleep that night.

"Mathew, how is Jenny?" Brown Bear asked. He knew that the man had his own responsibilities and would need to return to his own home.

"She woke this morning and ate and drank some of White Raven's tea. I'm confident she will be able to recover fully," Mathew said. Brown Bear nodded as he crossed his arms over his chest.

"There will be a parting ceremony tomorrow for the warriors that left this life last night in the battle. I hope you will be there with us to honor them," Brown Bear said.

"Of course, I will. I must return to the ranch to see to the cattle and Bailey. Daniel also needs a good rub down and to be fed. But I will return this afternoon to see to Jenny and her mother," he said.

"No rush, Mathew. I will make sure that the White women are well cared for. I very much like the idea of you and Jenny becoming one in the near future," Brown Bear said with a chuckle.

"One thing at a time, Brown Bear," Mathew said with a shake of his head. "But I would like that very much as well." The two parted then as Mathew collected his horses and headed towards his ranch. He wasn't sure when he'd be able to get a full night's rest again, but for now he was content with the knowledge that Jenny would live and recover from her injuries.

THE NEXT TIME Jenny came to, she saw her mother had risen as well and was now sitting close to the fire that had been built up. It burned brightly, filling the teepee with a welcoming warmth. Jenny lay quietly for a moment, slowly moving her arms and legs as she strove to stretch her sore muscles. She watched her mother and the concerned expression on her face.

"Never thought I'd ever sleep in a teepee," Jenny said. Margret came over immediately. She smiled brightly as she leaned over Jenny and hugged her gently.

"Oh, Jenny. I'm so glad to see you're awake and alive," Margret said as tears came to her eyes. She was overjoyed to see Jenny's beautiful sky blue eyes looking up into hers once more. "I've been so worried about you."

"I'm doing okay, Mother. Really," Jenny said, hoping to reassure her. "I'm just a bit sore is all."

"I can only imagine what you must be feeling after everything you went through," Margret said as she brushed back Jenny's hair, wanting to never let her out of her sight again. She knew that the thought was foolish, but it was simply how she felt at this moment. She knew that she couldn't blame Mathew for what had happened to her daughter, but she was still unsettled by the fact that harm had come to Jenny.

"I will recover soon enough and then we can return to cleaning and attempting to cook," Jenny said with a chuckle. They laughed together as Margret looked down at her daughter lovingly.

"I don't know how soon we'll be able to return to the ranch because of your injury," Margret said honestly. "But I don't exactly feel comfortable here."

Jenny nodded, knowing it must feel so strange to be in an Indian camp. "I will try my best to recovery quickly," Jenny said.

"You just need to rest is all," Margret said firmly. "And I will find us something to eat...eventually." Margret didn't want to admit that she was frightened of the Indians and didn't even feel comfortable leaving the teepee. But she also knew that she couldn't hide forever and would need to leave the teepee if only to take care of her personal needs.

The sound of a scratch coming against the teepee flap attracted their attention. "What is it?" Margret called out, startled by the sound.

Jenny watched as Brown Bear then pulled back the flap and entered before pulling it shut again and sitting on the ground by the door.

"Hello, I am Brown Bear, Chief of this Sioux Tribe," Brown Bear explained to the woman he'd met briefly the night before. "How are you doing, Jenny?"

"I am well, Brown Bear, thank you," Jenny said, wishing that she was sitting up.

"I am glad to see so," Brown Bear replied. "May I allow the women to come and tend to your needs?" Margret and Jenny were surprised to hear this and to think the Indians would be so generous.

"Brown Bear, I don't want to be a burden to any one," Jenny quickly said. Brown Bear smiled, kindness in his eyes.

"You are not a burden, Jenny. We are only sorry that you were hurt," he said. "The other women that were captured said that you tried to fight the attackers off and that is how you were hurt so badly." Margret looked at her daughter then, very concerned at hearing this.

"I was so frightened, Brown Bear, that I was willing to do anything to get away from them," Jenny said.

Brown Bear nodded. He knew what it was like to fear for one's own life and to fight with all your might to survive. "You were very brave, Jenny. And many of the Indian maidens would like to show their appreciation to you. It is not often that a maiden fights in battle," Brown Bear explained with a smile.

"It's still hard to believe that you went through all of that only last night," Margret said as she moved her hand through her daughter's hair, tears coming to her eyes at the thought of almost losing her.

"Fear not, Mrs. Phillips," Brown Bear tried to reassure her. "Jenny will receive the best care while she's in camp with us." Margret only nodded, not wanting to be rude by stating the fact that she wasn't kept safe to begin with. But now wasn't the time to voice her anger. She understood that the Indians were only protecting themselves, and now they'd even offered to tend to them.

"Thank you, Brown Bear. We'd appreciate any assistance," Jenny said for her mother. Brown Bear nodded, satisfied with Jenny's response. He grunted his approval before quickly leaving the teepee to let the women know their assistance was welcome.

Moments later, several maidens came into the teepee with smiles on their faces and different bundles in their hands. Margret moved over to the other side of her daughter, her back against the wall of the teepee as she watched in awe and wonder. A few began to cook on the central fire while others started to remove the furs from Jenny and help her into a sitting position. It was a bit painful, but Jenny was glad for the assistance. In time, she was helped into new clothes that were gifted to her from the Indian women, but first she was bathed with cool strips of linen that were soaked in a clay pot of water.

"It's miraculous how generous they are," Margret spoke up at one point. She was feeling better after enjoying flat bread with spices for breakfast. "We can't understand each other, yet we can still work together."

"I find it quite fascinating," Jenny said, enjoying the soft fabric of the buck skin dress against her skin. With a pair of leggings to go with it, Jenny was starting to feel better than she had in a while. Her long auburn hair had even been combed and braided, and Jenny was thinking of how she'd like to pay back their hospitality in the future.

After a while, the maidens helped Jenny to stand and led her and Margret to a place where they could take care of their calls of nature. Jenny and Margret giggled about it, feeling quite adventurous. But Jenny was simply glad to be able to stretch her legs because she'd felt so sore for so long. The day was cold, but the air felt refreshing as she moved about slowly with the help of the Indian women. She even settled herself on a log by the central fire with several furs wrapped around her and her mother as they simply sat and watched all the Indians moving about them.

Jenny watched curiously as many Indians constructed several large platforms on the far side of the Indian camp. They were about eight feet above the ground. Jenny wondered what the platforms were being made for. Each was perfectly created from several branches and logs bound together and supported by long branches. She was concentrating so hard on watching the Indians work that she didn't even realize that Brown Bear had settled down next to her and her mother on the log.

"They are building tree scaffolds for the burial of the many Indian braves that were killed last night," Brown Bear said as he noticed the way Jenny and Mrs. Phillips were watching the construction of the platforms with curiosity. The White women looked at him, sorrow clearly in their eyes.

"I'm so sorry to hear that, Brown Bear," Margret said. "I did not realize how many people had died last night."

Brown Bear nodded, appreciating the woman's sympathies. "There were many, but the Sioux believe that death is only the beginning of a journey into the Spirit World," he explained. "Though it is sad to see our family go, we are still joyful for their journey and sacrifice. They will be clothed in their best garments and placed upon the platforms with their possessions. Then tomorrow, they will all be burned, and their spirits set free to travel onto the next life."

Jenny didn't know what to say. The idea of seeing the platforms with their burdens set aflame didn't settle well with her. But she had to respect their customs and traditions. With having so recently lost her father, she tried to imagine what it would be like to see him upon one of these platforms, in his best business suit, and his most loved possessions around him. She preferred knowing that her father had been laid to rest in the church's cemetery.

"We buried my husband a few months ago," Margret said. She hadn't talked about her husband's death since it happened and didn't know why she was talking to an Indian chief about such things. She figured that a part of her simply wanted Brown Bear to know that she understood what it meant to lose someone you loved dearly.

"Then perhaps tomorrow you'd like to join us for the memorial ceremony? If you have something of your husband's, we could make a platform for him, too," Brown Bear offered. Margret smiled at the man as she shook her head.

"That is not necessary, Brown Bear," she replied. "But I do appreciate your continued kindness." Brown Bear only nodded once, not wanting to press the invitation to the women. He was reminded once again how different his people were from the White settlers. He was grateful to be able to interact with them, and even to learn their language. But there would always be some things that he simply didn't understand about the White people.

"The maidens will come soon to prepare the afternoon meal," Brown Bear said. "Mrs. Phillips, would you care to join them?" A glint of humor came to Brown Bear's eyes as he looked down at the older woman. He was curious to see how she'd react.

"Well, I'm always willing to try new things. I do love to cook and perhaps I could learn something new," Margret agreed. She didn't want to refuse another offer from Brown Bear and could agree to a cooking lesson.

As Brown Bear had indicated, soon several maidens started coming around the central fire. All manner of work seemed to cease as many of the Indians began to gather. But unlike last night when many would smile at Jenny, most seemed to be sorrowing for someone they'd lost, or looked towards her and Margret with concern on their faces. Jenny couldn't blame how they felt now towards White people. After all, a group of them had attacked last night.

But faces seemed to soften as Margret got up from the log with a fur wrapped around her shoulders as she neared the fire and began to help the maidens. Meat was cut and added with different root vegetables into a clay pot. Water from the nearby stream was added with different spices Margret had never even smelled before. She understood they were making some sort of stew and was happy to help. The large open fire filled Margret with such warmth that soon she was shrugging off the fur.

Jenny enjoyed watching her mother with the Indian women. Though they were two different people with customs that were very much foreign to her and her mother, it was good to see Margret around other women. She knew that it did her mother good to socialize as often as possible, and working in town had surely added to her mother's good health. Jenny smiled as she watched her mother work, smelling the wonderful aromas as clay pots were then pushed under the hot coals of the burning fire.

"I might have dirtied my gown, but I think the job is done," Margret said to her daughter as she returned to her side. A happy glow radiated from her face. A part of it was from working so close to the fire, but part was from having learned new cooking.

"I think I might actually be hungry," Jenny said as her mother settled down next to her on the log. "It smells good, whatever it is."

"Looks to be some sort of stew or roast," Margret explained. The women had started to fry more flat bread and the area was soon filled with pleasant aromas and idle chatter.

When a horse came trotting into camp, many stood. They looked spooked and on edge, but as Jenny watched, she saw Mathew making his way through the teepees as he settled his horse into the corral with the Indian ponies. Jenny was happy to see him, his dog Bailey following after him. Once Bailey caught sight of Jenny, the collie zipped around everyone and came dashing over to her, wanting to climb onto her lap and give her lots of kisses.

"Bailey, no!" Mathew said as he chased after the dog. Bailey obeyed the calling of his master and quickly laid down underneath Jenny's legs as though he was sorry for what he'd done. "Are you okay, Jenny?"

"Yes, I am fine," Jenny said with a chuckle. "I didn't think Bailey would be so happy to see me."

"I think he's gotten used to seeing you around the house and was worried when you didn't come home," Mathew said as he sat next to Jenny on the log. "How are you two doing?"

"We are fine, Mathew," Margret said. "The Indian women have been very kind and generous."

Mathew was pleased to hear this, and even a bit surprised that Mrs. Phillips had addressed him using his first name. "That is good news. My goodness, something smells good," Mathew said as he looked towards the fire.

"Mother helped the women prepare the afternoon meal," Jenny said with a smile. "She says that it's some sort of stew."

"Well, I'm sure it's going to be tastier with Mrs. Phillips adding her touch to it," Mathew said towards the older woman. Margret just chuckled as she shook her head.

"I don't know about that," Margret said. After a while, bowls of stew with pieces of fresh flat bread were passed to everyone who was sitting around the central fire. Children who'd been quiet all day seemed to brighten at seeing Bailey in camp. The collie eventually made his way out from under Jenny's legs as he ventured around the circle, licking the faces of the children as they all crowded around him to pet his fur coat.

"Someone is sure popular," Jenny said as she motioned towards the dog. Mathew laughed as he looked at his dog, the sound of his laughter very pleasing to Jenny. She watched him, thinking how lucky she was to be alive in order to enjoy his company.

"Bailey always attracts all the kids in the village. Indians don't keep pets," Mathew explained. Soon, the kids were chasing Bailey around the camp as the dog playfully ran away from them, circling back to run right past them. It was a fun game of chase and tag as the laughter of children filled the air. Jenny thought how wonderful it would be to one day have children of her own and listen to the sound of their laughter. The idea was a bit startling, but a comforting one, none-theless.

After the meal was done, both Mathew and Margret helped Jenny to walk back to the teepee they'd been given to allow Jenny time to rest and heal. She was feeling awfully tired, and after a good meal, she was eager to lay down again. Being under the pile of furs felt like the safest place in the world. It didn't take long before she drifted off to sleep, the idea of Mathew and her mother close by bringing her much peace.

# CHAPTER 14

$\mathcal{A}$ sadness filled Mathew as he stood behind the crowd of Indians as everyone gathered for the memorial ceremony for those Indian braves that had lost their lives. To his right stood Jenny and her mother, both wrapped in their cloaks and furs. The day was bitterly cold and matched how most felt in camp. During his time there yesterday afternoon, he could tell that many hearts had hardened towards White people. He'd spoken to Brown Bear about the matter, and both had agreed that no one could blame them for how they felt.

Now, Mathew stood and watched as personal items were placed upon the platforms with the bodies of those that had died in battle. Treasured knives and bow and arrows were placed as part of the personal items along with other things the warriors might need in the next phase of their eternal lives. The deceased had been dressed in their finest clothes and covered with furs as though they were still alive. A song for which Mathew did not know the words soon rose in the crowd. But even though the words were foreign to him, he still tried to hum to the rhythm to respect those that had passed on.

Jenny was mesmerized by the ceremony. She was afraid that it would be off putting, but as she listened to the song that weaved its way through the crowd, she found it rather calming. When the platforms were set aflame, it didn't look gruesome like she'd imagined. Instead, it was almost like the flames rose simply to send the spirits of the deceased into the air and onwards towards the next life.

When the song stopped, people started to depart. No one looked back as Brown Bear led the procession away from the platforms and instead to the central fire. There, a large celebration seemed to take place. Food was prepared, singing and dancing commenced, and Jenny sat next to Mathew as her mother helped out where she could. Margret wanted to be as helpful as possible since the Indians had been so kind to her and Jenny these last few days. She was also enjoying working alongside the older women in making a meal for everyone.

"Your mother seems to be really settling into the area," Mathew said. He felt melancholy after the memorial service and wanted to lift his spirits by talking to Jenny about what had been on his mind lately.

"She really is," Jenny said with a smile. Her shoulder was really starting to hurt but she was enjoying her time with Mathew. "I am glad to see her so well after such a long time of feeling the pain of my father's death." Mathew nodded, knowing what it was like to lose both parents.

"I hope you two will remain here in Bear Creek, even after what's happened here at the camp," Mathew said, hoping that what Jenny had gone through hadn't changed her mind about remaining.

"Of course, we will," Jenny said as she looked up at Mathew, a small smile on her face. "As soon as I'm able, we'll be back at the ranch and back to work in town." Mathew felt such relief that he let out a deep sigh. Jenny watched him closely, wondering how he was feeling about her. After going through such a terrifying experience, certain things had come into perspective for her.

"Mathew, what I went through I wouldn't wish on my worst enemy," Jenny ended up saying as she gathered her courage. Mathew looked at her, their eyes meeting as his filled with concern for her.

"I'm glad to be alive and it's really helped me see what is most important in my life."

"I can't begin to understand what you must be feeling after all of this," Mathew said.

"Well, one thing I've come to realize is just how much I like you," Jenny said, smiling. She was nervous about how Mathew would react, and soon her cheeks were burning with a deep blush.

Mathew was stunned by her words. He wasn't expecting her to say anything like this to him so close to almost dying. But it filled him with excitement and happiness to know that she felt the same way he did.

"I really like you too, Jenny. I didn't want to put any pressure on you since you're still recovering, but when you do feel better, I want to officially start courting you," Mathew said with a bright smile. They looked deep into each other's eyes, feeling more happiness than either one had felt in a long time.

"I'd agree to that, Mathew," Jenny finally said. "I would like that very much." Mathew was so thrilled that he didn't know what to do. Instead, he wrapped his arm around Jenny while being careful not to interfere with her injured shoulder. He pulled her closer to him, enjoying the warmth that filled his body to have her so close, and to know that she shared his feelings for her.

Though Margret had been busy helping with the meal, singing and dancing going on all around her, she'd still kept an eye on Jenny. And when she saw Mathew place his arm around her and the way they looked at each other, she could tell that something special had passed between them. She smiled at the sight of the young couple together, hoping that Jenny would finally find the one person she could fall in love with and marry one day. It would give Margret peace of mind to see Jenny settled so well after everything they'd been through.

AFTER A FEW MORE DAYS OF rest at camp, Jenny and her mother were finally ready to try to venture back to the ranch. During the daytime, Mathew had tended to his cattle and continued his preparations for winter. But he'd also tried to make sure the house stayed tidy so that when Jenny and Margret returned, they wouldn't feel pressured to clean too much. He was looking forward to their cooking again and only hoped that Jenny would feel at ease at the house.

One afternoon, Mathew went to camp with both his draft horse and mare. He thought that Margret could ride back on Buttercup, and Jenny would be able to ride double with him. Mathew reasoned that if Jenny sat in front on the saddle, he could help to keep her stable while they traveled. At least, that was the plan that Mathew had come up with. As he got into camp, he settled the horses near the corral and then went in search of the Phillips women.

The breath was taken from Mathew's lungs as he found the women outside of the teepee Jenny had been resting in. She was still in the Indian clothing she'd been given, showcasing how lovely her body was, but now her hair had been braided in several strands and pulled back in a way that it looked like her hair formed a halo above her head. He thought she was absolutely breath taking, and it took him some time to regain his composure before he could join them amongst all the Indian maidens.

"Hello ladies," Mathew said in greeting. Jenny's face brightened at seeing him, and for a moment they looked deeply into one another's eyes.

Jenny had worn many elegant gowns to balls that were made from silk and adorned with lace. But she never felt as beautiful as she did now in a long Indian gown with leggings underneath. She almost didn't like the idea of dressing in her normal day gown and wondered how often she'd be able to wear the clothing that had been gifted to her. As she looked into Mathew's eyes, she could tell that he also appreciated her clothing.

"Hello, Mathew," Margret said when her daughter failed to say anything. The other women giggled as they watched the young couple. Language wasn't needed to help explain how the two of them felt for one another.

"The horses are ready to take you two back to the ranch," Mathew explained. "Mrs. Phillips, I'll lead you like last time on Buttercup. Jenny can ride double with me. I hope if she rides in front, she'll feel more stable."

"Sounds like a good enough plan," Margret said. "I think we should say goodbye to Brown Bear before we go."

"Yes, I would like to thank him for all his kindness," Jenny said, seeming to finally find her voice. Jenny then turned to the Indian women who had been so kind to her these last few days, and she took the time to gently hug each one of them before departing. It still hurt her shoulder to lift her arm, but she wanted to show these women just how much she appreciated each and every one of them. A few even took the time to hug her mother, which Jenny found amusing because she knew that her mother wasn't much of a hugger.

Once they'd said their goodbyes to the women, the three made their way to Brown Bear's teepee. As Mathew scratched on the side, they were surprised when Brown Bear stepped out with Sheriff Benning right behind him. Mathew was instantly concerned once he saw Jacob and was worried that something else had happened.

"Seems like you two are ready to head home," Brown Bear said as he faced the White women. "Jenny, it has been a pleasure to have you and your mother with us. You two are welcome in camp anytime."

"Thank you, Brown Bear. One day, I shall repay your kindness," Jenny said with much determination.

Brown Bear chuckled as he nodded. "You have a strong spirit, Jenny. I have no doubt that you are bound by your word," Brown Bear said, pleased to hear her words. "And Mrs. Phillips, you must join us often. I believe the women enjoyed your company."

"I'll be sure to visit when time allows," Margret said. She had honestly enjoyed her time in camp but wasn't sure how she'd be able to return on her own. She wasn't looking forward to riding a horse back to the ranch but understood that she had very little option. She certainly wasn't going to walk the whole way back.

"Jacob," Mathew said as he nodded towards him. "I hope you've come bearing good news." Mathew had waited patiently for the women to say their goodbyes, but the longer he waited, the more impatient he became.

"I've come to talk to Brown Bear about Geoffrey and his men. I've been able to officially close down the mines with the approval of Montana's marshal. Geoffrey won't be able to open them again until he pays restitution to Brown Bear and his people for the several deaths they caused," Jacob explained. He'd done all he could to stick to the Indian customs, while also making sure that a man like Geoffrey never saw the light of day again.

"And since the man is pretty much broke, he's signed the land deed over to me. I can't believe the thing was actually real," Jacob added. Mathew was surprised to hear this, but at least glad that Brown Bear and his people wouldn't have to leave Bear Creek.

"What do you plan to do with the land deed?" Mathew asked as he looked towards Brown Bear. The older man smiled at him, mischief seeming to shine in his eyes.

"I will sign it over to Brown Bear when he becomes eligible to own land as the government sees fit. Till then, I'll just keep it locked up at the Sheriff's Office," Jacob said with a smile on his face. Mathew couldn't help but smile also as he thought how good an idea that was. Brown Bear might never be able to own land, but at least his land was protected as long as Jacob didn't get any wrong ideas.

"Furthermore, Geoffrey and his remaining men are being transferred up north to the big jail," Jacob said. "We won't have to worry about those crooked miners causing any more trouble around these parts."

"But that also means the town will truly suffer from the mine being officially closed," Mathew said. He was glad to hear that the Indians wouldn't have to worry about the miners bothering them anymore, but Bear Creek was already hurting for business.

"Perhaps one day someone will buy the mines and bring good workers back to town," Jenny added, hoping to lift everyone's spirits with her words. Mathew smiled at her, loving how optimistic Jenny always was.

"We'll see," was all that Jacob said as he tipped his Stetson to the group before making his way to his horse and heading back to town. He had to meet back up with Tanner so they could arrange the transportation of their criminals.

"Well, Brown Bear. We're going to be off now. Thank you for everything you've done for the women," Mathew said as he turned back to the Indian Chief.

"It was my pleasure, Mathew. Do not be a stranger to us in the future, even with winter settling into these lands," Brown Bear replied. He grunted his goodbye before dipping back into his teepee. He had much to discuss with the elders of his tribe about the future of Bear Creek.

Mathew chuckled as he turned to the women. "We better be off then," he said as he led them over to the horses. First, Mathew helped Mrs. Phillips up into the saddle of Buttercup. She was much more graceful than the last time, but Jenny still chuckled at her mother.

"You look good on the horse, Mother," Jenny said, trying to be encouraging.

"Does not matter if I look good, Jenny. I must learn to ride a horse so I can come visit my new friends," Margret said with much determination. She held onto the saddle horn as she adjusted herself, ordering her feet in the stirrups before she motioned for Mathew to hand her the reins.

"Don't you want me to lead Buttercup?" Mathew asked, surprised by her request.

"No, I must learn to do this myself," Margret said, confident in her decision. Mathew relented after seeing how determined Margret was. After giving her some instructions, he then helped Jenny up into Daniel's saddle, having her move slowly and easily so that she didn't bump her shoulder too much. Then, he pulled himself up behind her, making sure she was comfortable before they took off.

Mathew set off through camp as a few Indians stopped to say their goodbyes as well. Several waved goodbye, while others watched them go without moving a muscle. Mathew knew that it would take time before everyone in the Indian camp had rekindled their trust with the locals in Bear Creek. But for now, Mathew was simply content to know that the Indians wouldn't be bothered by the miners any longer.

Mathew led the horses through camp at a slow pace, and even slower once they crossed the tree line and followed the narrow path towards his ranch. Occasionally he'd look behind him to see how Mrs. Phillips was faring. She had a determined expression on her face but seemed to be doing well enough. Buttercup stayed close to Daniel as they made their way through the forest. Mathew kept one arm around Jenny, his hand on the saddle horn and the other holding the reins as they traveled. He had to admit that he was enjoying being this close to Jenny. He took a deep breath, savoring her sweet smell. He was truly grateful to have her in his life and hoped that they would have a successful courtship.

Traveling through the forest had the same magical effect on Jenny as the first time she'd ridden through it as she looked all around. The high sun cast plenty of light through the tops of the trees, rays of sunlight falling everywhere around them. The forest seemed to be alive as birds flew all around, chirping happily. As they crossed the creek, the sounds she'd heard before from the miners was no longer there. She felt that the forest had returned to a more natural state without the miners presence.

As they traveled, Jenny tried to stay with the rhythm of the horse. She felt safe with Mathew at her back. If her mother wasn't nearby, she might have also enjoyed this close contact more. But she knew that her mother would be watching their every move, so Jenny kept her hands to her side of the saddle as Mathew kept his arm around her, hand holding onto the saddle horn and thus keeping them secured in place. She couldn't deny that she was enjoying having Mathew's arm around her and felt she could travel like this forever.

But eventually they made it back to the ranch. Bailey was there to greet them, barking happily as they came onto the ranch and into the barn to put the horses away. Mathew descended first before helping Jenny down, and then assisted her mother.

"You rode that horse like a pro, Mrs. Phillips," Mathew complimented as he took Buttercup's reins and led the mare into her stall so she could rest and be fed.

"Please, Mathew. Call me Margret," she replied with a proud smile. She'd been nervous about riding a horse, but now felt more confident about doing it again in the future. Margret stepped over to Jenny and placed an arm around her as she began to lead her daughter into the house. Mathew was surprised by Mrs. Phillips' offer to call her by her first name but reasoned that it was a step in the right direction. With her approval, he'd be able to ask Jenny to marry him one day.

Mathew was quick to get Buttercup settled before he led Daniel to the house. He tethered the draft horse there before heading inside the house. He wanted to make sure Jenny was settled before heading out to the pasture to check in with the cattle. Bailey walked beside him as he ducked inside the house, seeing Margret easing Jenny down into a chair near the fireplace.

"My goodness, Mathew. You've certainly kept the place up," Margret said as she placed an afghan over Jenny before making her way to the kitchen. She reasoned she would put something together for dinner easily now that she'd had plenty of practice.

"Thank you, Margret," Mathew said, testing out the woman's name. She smiled pleasantly back at him as she started to busy herself in the kitchen. She was happy to be back in the ranch house and looked forward to sleeping in a real bed. Though she'd been comfortable in the Indian camp, there was nothing quite like a real house to make her feel truly at ease. She was even starting to see that ranch house more as her home now that they were becoming settled in Bear Creek.

As Margret left them alone, Mathew went to kneel beside Jenny as she sat in the chair, her eyes already seeming to close shut with exhaustion.

"I'll be out in the pastures for the rest of the day, but I'll be back in for dinner and to help you with anything you need," Mathew promised as he took her hand and rubbed his thumb over the back of her hand. He wasn't sure if this was being too forward since they'd only just agreed to start courting, but it felt good to hold her hand in his.

"There's no rush, Mathew. I'm just going to take a bit of a rest and then I'm sure I'll be able to help Mother with dinner," Jenny said, her eyes closed as she rested her head against the wingback chair. She loved the feeling of Mathew's hand in hers and wished she could spend the rest of the day simply holding his hand.

"Get some rest," Mathew said before letting go of her hand and making his way out of the ranch house. As Mathew climbed back up into Daniel's saddle, he turned the horse towards the pasture and whistled for Bailey to follow him. They had work to do and already he'd spent too much time away from his ranch. But as he rode away from the house, he was at least content to know that Jenny was safe at the ranch house and would be making a full recovery in a matter of days.

Seeming to finally have overcome the terrible ordeal, Mathew looked forward to spending more time with Jenny and working towards courting her properly.

# CHAPTER 15

It took some time before Jenny felt ready enough to travel to town with her mother so they could fulfill the employment opportunities they'd agreed to. For the last few days, her mother had been traveling to town alone after Jenny helped her hitch Buttercup to the wagon. It hadn't been an easy process to master and they had laughed together over the difficulties before they decided that without Mathew to check they'd got everything right. It was better for Margret to ride Buttercup into town on her own with her small bag of cleaning supplies. Now that Jenny was feeling up to the trip, Margret was looking forward to spending time with her daughter once more.

Just the night before Jenny had finally told her mother that she and Mathew would finally be officially courting. Margret had been pleased beyond belief to hear the good news, even though she'd suspected as such. And with things becoming romantic between Jenny and Mathew, Margret did her best to stay out of their way by retiring early for bed to give the young couple some time alone.

Jenny looked forward to spending her evenings alone with Mathew. Though her mother was just down the hallway, no doubt still awake, Jenny and Mathew had simply sat around the fire, talking about all manner of things. At first, Mathew often talked about his work with the cattle and what he had been trying to accomplish that day. And then Jenny would explain what she'd felt able to do that day and how her shoulder had been feeling. Dr. Harvey had paid her a house visit a few days back to check on her wound and had declared that everything was healing properly but that she'd have a scar on her back for the rest of her life.

Jenny was just thankful that life was returning back to normal in some ways. She wasn't upset about having a scar and figured it could have been a lot worse. Instead, she was able to look forward to growing stronger each day and more capable of taking care of herself. She wanted to become the independent woman that she'd aspired to be, and now she felt like she could accomplish that goal as she traveled to town with her mother.

"Do you think we'll be able to do this once it starts to snow?" Margret asked her daughter who'd become deep in thought.

"I sure hope so, Mother. We'll need the money for the things we'll need during the winter. Mathew told me the other night that Mr. Fry will raise his prices during the winter because supplies will become quite scarce," Jenny said. "And I haven't even thought to see if there is anything left in Mathew's garden."

"Let us worry about that tomorrow," Margret said reassuringly. She knew that Mathew had been working hard to stock the pantry and cellar for the winter months, and she didn't worry that they'd starve to death even if it snowed and kept them indoors for several days. "We'll see to the garden in the morning." Jenny simply nodded as she led Buttercup into town. She was looking forward to seeing some familiar faces and getting back to work.

When they got into town, the first place they stopped was Mr. and Mrs. Tibet's inn. After pulling Buttercup to a halt outside the inn, Margret and Jenny put a large blanket over the horse to keep her warm, then they made their way inside. They were both looking forward to warming up inside and getting to work.

"Ah, Jenny! It's so good to see you again," Mr. Tibet said as they came into the inn. He stood behind the counter and came around to greet them.

"Hello, Mr. Tibet," Jenny said as she took off her bonnet. Already she felt much warmer inside the inn. "I apologize for not being able to come by last week."

"Oh, nonsense." Mr. Tibet waved his hand at her as to suggest it had all been no big deal. "We all heard about what those nasty miners did. Not saying I'm an Indian lover, but it was still wrong to hurt those that can't defend themselves. I'm just so glad to see you after I heard you'd been hurt." Jenny smiled at the older man, always enjoying how he tended to ramble on when he had someone to listen to him.

"Why, thank you, Mr. Tibet," Jenny said as she and her mother hung up their cloaks and bonnets on the coat rack near the front door. "What rooms do you need tending to today?"

"We had several miners check out these last few days," Mr. Tibet said with a somber voice. "Many who weren't a part of the attack up and left town when Sheriff Benning closed down the mine. I have the room keys on the counter for you ladies."

"Great, we'll get started there and come back for anything else that might need tending to," Margret said in a cheerful voice. She didn't like having to talk about what had happened to her daughter but understood that this type of news would be the talk of the town for a long while. It was surely no different than when she'd lived in Richmond and any scandalous news could circulate for weeks.

"Very good. I'm sure the rooms are not in the best condition since they'd been rented out for so long. So, I'm willing to pay you two double for your work today," Mr. Tibet explained as he led the women over to the counter and handed them several room keys. Jenny was surprised by how many there were and was concerned that Mr. Tibet wouldn't be able to afford to pay them if they had no more guests. But instead of trying to protest, she simply smiled because she knew that she and her mother could use the money.

"Thank you, Mr. Tibet. That is very kind of you," Margret said. Once Jenny had the keys in her apron pocket, they bid Mr. Tibet farewell for the time being and made their way upstairs to tend to the rooms.

As they came to the first room, Jenny found the correct key and opened the door. The stench of mold and decay hit them in the face as they peered into the room. The curtains had been drawn over the windows and the room was dark.

"Men can be such pigs sometimes," Jenny said with a huff. She walked into the room, mindful of the bedding that had been tossed on the floor, and quickly pulled back the curtains and opened the window for some fresh air.

"My goodness, what a mess." Margret slowly came into the room and gazed all about with disgust on her face. All the bed linen had been soiled as though the miner had returned from the hills and plopped onto the bed without even taking the time to shower. Soot and mud were all over the floor, bed, and furniture as dirty clothes had been slung over the back of the chairs.

"This is going to take us all day," Jenny said, her voice a bit discouraged. She knew she wasn't fully recovered and the work ahead of them seemed to be overwhelming. And if there were several other rooms in this same condition, she wondered if they would be able to get it all done in the same day.

"Chin up, Jenny. We're going to do this together and do a good job, too," Margret said to her daughter, not liking the way she sounded so defeated. It wasn't like Jenny to ever voice her fears or concerns, and she hoped that being attacked hadn't dampened her spirits any.

Jenny nodded towards her mother and put a smile on for her. She'd been faced with bigger problems before and wouldn't let this small obstacle get in her way. After all, Mr. Tibet was willing to pay them double for the work, and she certainly understood why now. Together Jenny and her mother, gathered all the soiled linens, including the curtains, and tossed them into the hallway.

"Might as well gather all the bedding before we can start on cleaning the furniture. The floors will have to be last," Jenny said as she started thinking of a plan of action.

"Good thinking," Margret replied. "Since you have the keys, gather all the soiled linens from the other rooms. Then we'll take everything to the end of the hallway and use the tub to clean everything."

As expected, the other rooms were just as messy as the first. But Jenny didn't let it dampen her spirits anymore. She worked hard to gather all the linens while keeping in mind that her shoulder still needed time to heal. She did her best not to agitate her shoulder as she moved slowly, yet efficiently.

As the day wore on, Mr. and Mrs. Tibet came to visit with them, giving them small breaks to chat and learn all of what had been happening in town since the last time they'd been able to ride in. Jenny and Margret both appreciated the distraction from their long list of work, and Mr. Tibet was always so amusing that laughing at his jokes often helped them to feel happy even when they were working hard. When lunch time came and the locals stopped in for a warm meal, Mrs. Tibet made sure to fix them both a bowl of hot chicken noodle soup that they ate in the kitchen with Mrs. Tibet since their day gowns had become quite dirty from all their hard work. But when the patrons heard that Jenny had recovered and had come in, they made time to stop and visit with her in the kitchen. Jenny felt so embarrassed to be so dirty from all the hard work, but she greatly appreciated everyone's kindness and consideration.

"This really is a close-knit community," Margret said to her daughter after lunch as they returned upstairs to finish their work. All the linens had been washed and hung outside despite the cooler temperature. The bedding wouldn't freeze, but it would take all day for everything to dry.

"It really is nice to see so many people come to check in on me," Jenny agreed. "I believe they were all equally concerned and simply not being nosey."

"What a breath of fresh air that is," Margret admitted. "People who genuinely care and not just wanting to catch a bit of rumor."

"I agree fully," Jenny said as they returned upstairs and began scrubbing clean all the furniture.

The day was long, but by the time they finished, both Jenny and Margret felt a great sense of accomplishment. What first seemed like an endless task had eventually been finished. Though the bedding and curtains were a bit stiff as they made all the beds and hung back up the curtains, at least they were thoroughly clean. The rooms certainly smelled fresher, and as Jenny closed and locked the last door before venturing back downstairs, she sighed with a huge sense of relief.

"I can't believe we finished," Jenny said as she followed her mother downstairs. Her shoulder was now hurting her pretty bad and she longed to return to the ranch to hopefully relax by the fire. She wasn't certain how much help she'd be to her mother tonight and hoped she didn't mind cooking alone.

"I knew we could do it," Margret said as she winked at her daughter. "We can accomplish anything we put our minds to." Jenny chuckled as she placed the room keys on the front counter. Mr. Tibet was serving the afternoon patrons in the dining area, and as they put on their bonnets and cloaks, he eventually made his way over to them.

"Give me one second. Mrs. Tibet has a surprise for you two," Mr. Tibet said with much enthusiasm as he went back into the kitchen. He returned moments later with a large basket. "Mrs. Tibet prepared a dinner meal for you three. We figured you two would be so exhausted from all your work that not having to worry about dinner would be nice."

"Oh, Mr. Tibet, how thoughtful," Margret said as she accepted the basket. She was surprised by how heavy it was and it felt warm in her hands. It would be lovely to hold it and stay warm while they traveled home.

"The payment for the day is in there, too," Mr. Tibet added.

"Thank you, Mr. Tibet," Jenny said. "We'll be sure to return it tomorrow when we come in to clean the bank."

"No rush. You two have a good evening and we'll see you Thursday," Mr. Tibet said in parting before returning to the kitchen to continue running orders. Jenny was pleased that at least people were still coming to the inn to enjoy a good meal. She hated to think that Mr. and Mrs. Tibet would be hard pressed because of lack of money from the miners.

With the basket in hand, they left the inn and made their way to the wagon. Buttercup looked happy to see them as she shook her mane. Jenny took a moment to pet her neck as she took off her blanket. Then the women climbed up into the wagon and started their way out of town.

"You know, Jenny," Margret said at one point during the journey home. "I'm really glad we decided to come all the way out here." Jenny smiled, feeling such relief to hear her mother say those words. She knew that the work they'd done that day had been unusually hard. It was much more than just housekeeping, and she wondered how it had affected her mother.

"Me too, Mother," Jenny replied as she held the reins in her hands. "I can't believe I'm driving a wagon or have just enjoyed an entire day of work."

"It is sometimes hard to believe we are where we are today compared to what our life used to be like," Margret agreed. "But I think the friendly people here really makes all the difference." Jenny immediately thought of Mathew and smiled. She was looking forward to returning to the ranch and getting to see him this evening.

"Yes, that is the best part of Bear Creek. Everyone is so friendly and helpful," Jenny said.

"And most of the men are good looking, too," Margret said, completely surprising her daughter. They both burst out into laughter till Jenny couldn't take the pain in her shoulder anymore. She grimaced as her shoulder began to throb. "My goodness, Jenny. Are you alright?"

"Yes, Mother. I just overdid it today," Jenny said as she tried to relax her hands without completely letting go of the reins. She was glad that Buttercup knew the way home and she didn't have to worry about the horse too much.

"Well, since we don't have to worry about making dinner tonight, I'll help prepare a bath for you," Margret said. "I'm sure a nice warm bath will help."

"That sounds wonderful, Mother," Jenny said as she sighed. Just the thought of having a nice warm bath made Jenny feel that much better.

$\mathcal{M}$athew had spent the day in the pasture with the cattle, driving them through the pasture to keep them warm and to make sure the herd was getting plenty of exercise. Bailey enjoyed running around the cattle, driving them and keeping them moving. Mathew couldn't help but chuckle as he watched his best friend run and prance around the cattle, beasts that were ten times bigger than the collie. Bailey reminded him a bit of Jenny who was filled with such fierceness that he looked forward to seeing just a glimpse of it every evening.

He was certainly curious to know how Jenny had fared that day. Mathew was worried that she might have overdone it with working in town today, but he wouldn't ever tell Jenny what to do. He understood that she was very independent, and he didn't want to ruin his chances of marriage by trying to tell her to rest instead of working. But even though he hadn't voiced his opinion, he was still very worried about her.

As the sun began to set and the day faded to night, Mathew whistled over to Bailey and together they made their way to the barn. Mathew felt a spark of excitement run through him when he saw that

Buttercup was in her stall and the wagon had been parked success-fully. That meant the women had returned and soon he'd be able to hear all about their day. After putting Daniel's saddle away and making sure both horses were brushed and fed for the night, he and Bailey made their way inside the ranch house.

The house was pleasantly warm as Mathew saw that the fire had been built back up since this morning. He hung up his coat and took off his boots at the door as Bailey bounded inside the house, barking excitedly. Bailey was quickly shushed by Margret as she came over from the kitchen. Bailey immediately sat on the floor as he wagged his tail at seeing a familiar face.

"Jenny is resting in her room," Margret said to the dog. "So, you must be quiet."

"Is she feeling okay?" Mathew quickly asked.

"Oh yes, just exhausted," Margret said reassuringly. "The inn was such a mess after all the miners left. We really had our work cut out for us today."

Margret made her way back into the kitchen where she was reheating their dinner on the stove. Mrs. Tibet had prepared them a large shepherd's pie to enjoy, along with her famous peach cobbler. Margret's mouth watered as the sweet and savory aromas filled the house.

"So, I'm guessing all the miners who weren't involved in the attack also left town," Mathew said as he came towards the kitchen to help out where he could. He started to set the table, looking forward to tonight's meal.

"In a hurry is an understatement. Those rooms were soiled completely," Margret said with a huff. "I'm glad Jenny and I were able to do the work, but we had to take thorough baths when we came home. And I think Jenny over-did it a bit." Mathew grimaced at the thought. He was pleased that the Phillips women had work, but he was worried about Jenny's well-being as she continued to recover.

"White Raven gave me some tea to make for Jenny in case she was ever in pain," Mathew said. "I'll make her some right now." Margret smiled as she nodded.

"I think she'd enjoy that very much," she agreed. Margret put the kettle on the stove after filling it from the buckets she'd filled earlier from the well. As it began to boil, Mathew took the small pouch White Raven had given him and placed some of the herbs in the bottom of a tin cup before filling it up with the hot water. Once it had cooled a little, he passed it to Margret.

"It should be ready by now," Mathew said.

Margret shook her head as she looked at Mathew. "Why don't you take it in to her," she suggested.

"You wouldn't mind?" Mathew asked, surprised by the offer.

"I don't mind at all," Margret assured him with a smile. "She's decent, and I'm sure she'd enjoy the company. That and she needs to wake up for dinner."

Not wanting to argue with the woman, Mathew simply nodded and slowly walked with the hot cup of tea to Jenny's room. He knocked a few times on the door before opening it. And before Mathew could say anything, Bailey dashed into the room and jumped onto the bed before settling down by Jenny's feet. Jenny woke then and chuckled once she saw Bailey. Seeing that the woman was awake, Bailey inched his way towards her till she could reach down and pet him.

"He acts like he's so spoiled," Mathew said as he came into the room. He left the door wide open so that the room would not only be warmed, but so Margret could keep an eye on them if she wanted to.

"That is because he is spoiled," Jenny said as she yawned and sat up in the bed. "Bailey sleeps in a bed and everything." Mathew simply shrugged his shoulders, knowing she spoke the truth. He then pulled over a chair to the side of the bed and sat next to Jenny.

"Here is some willow bark tea I made you. White Raven explained that it would help with your pain. Margret said that you two had a rough day," Mathew said as he handed Jenny the tin mug. She gladly accepted it and took a few small sips. The taste was very unpleasant but she was simply happy to have something to help dull the pain in her shoulder.

"I think the inn was a complete mess until we were finished," Jenny said. "It was like those men never took the time to bathe."

"I could understand since they worked underground every day," Mathew reasoned. "What's the point of bathing when you were just going to get covered in dirt the very next day?"

"Well, it's one thing to bring dirt into your own home instead of making someone else's that filthy," Jenny said with a chuckle. "It's like they plopped down on their bed as soon as they returned to the inn." Mathew simply shook his head, unable to imagine just how dirty the inn rooms had been.

"I'm glad at least to see you resting," Mathew said, wanting to change the subject. "I had been worried about you all day since I wasn't sure how the work would affect your shoulder." Jenny smiled at Mathew over the rim of the tin cup as she took a few more sips.

"You were worried about me, were you?" Jenny asked as she flirted with him a bit. She was curious to see how romantically compatible they were. Mathew chuckled in response as he nodded, his brown hair moving around his face. It looked like it was growing long again.

"I will not deny that I was thoroughly worried," Mathew admitted. "When I returned to the ranch house and Margret said you were resting, it only added to my worry that something had happened during the day while you were in town." Jenny appreciated his concern, but like the others she'd spoken to that day, she wanted to put his worries to rest.

"It will take time to fully heal, but I was fine today. I'm sure the inn rooms won't be that dirty every time we go in," Jenny said. "It was just a hard day, and sometimes days are going to be like that. But you never have to worry about me."

Mathew smiled as he listened to her. "I can't promise I'll ever stop worrying," he said as he looked deeply into her eyes. Even in the fading sunlight, they sparked a bright blue. Jenny thought she could remain like this forever, simply becoming lost in the depths of Mathew's hazel eyes. But eventually they were interrupted when Margret popped in to say that dinner was ready. Bailey bounded off the bed, eager for his meal. Jenny and Mathew chuckled as they watched the dog trot after Margret.

"Well, I'll meet you out there," Mathew said as he rose from the chair and gave Jenny a moment alone. She smiled sweetly at him as he left and closed the door behind him. Jenny then pushed back the blankets and got up from the bed before putting on her house slippers. She finished the cup of tea and hoped that the herbs would take away the pain soon. Lighting a candle with a box of matches, she then made her way slowly to the main room.

Jenny left her candle in the kitchen as she set her empty tin cup in the sink and then went to sit down at the table. She inhaled deeply, the pleasant aromas of dinner filling her nose and making her hungry all of a sudden.

"Mrs. Tibet made her special shepherd's pie and peach cobbler for us," Margret explained as she began to dish out portions for them all.

"That woman is a God send," Jenny said as she accepted a plate of food. It looked delicious and she couldn't wait to try a bite. But she waited patiently for Mathew to say grace before they began to eat.

"Mrs. Tibet certainly out did herself this time," Mathew said during the course of the dinner. He always enjoyed Mrs. Tibet's cooking and it was a pleasant surprise to find out that the older woman had sent home dinner with Margret and Jenny. He was certainly grateful since he knew that Jenny wasn't feeling well. But as he watched her eat, he was happy to see that at least she had a good appetite.

"Mother, we should try to bake a few things this week to repay Mrs. Tibet's kindness, and also take something to the camp," Jenny suggested. "We have plenty from what Mr. Tibet paid us today." Margret smiled at her daughter as she nodded.

"I'll get the cookbook out tonight and we can discuss it," Margret agreed.

Mathew enjoyed watching the two chatter happily about cooking.

The two of them had really shown him how to find joy in the simplest of things. Cooking for himself had always seemed like a chore because it was one of the last things he did for himself at the end of a long day, and normally he just threw something together real fast to simply get through another day. But the Phillips women had shown him how enjoyable eating a meal together could be, and that when you work together you are able to accomplish more than you ever thought possible.

After so many years of living alone, his heart felt full to have Margret and Jenny staying with him. He was truly developing strong feelings for Jenny and couldn't wait to see how things would turn out between them. He had an idea for what to do with Jenny the next day she had off from work, and this time they would be able to stay close to the ranch. He surely felt more protective over Jenny and wanted to show her that Bear Creek could also be a fun place to live in.

Once the dinner was over and the dishes had been cleaned up afterwards, Jenny settled down into a chair near the fire. Margret soon bid them goodnight before Mathew came and joined Jenny. For a few minutes, Jenny simply looked into the fire, grateful for the warmth. She knew that she had many things to be grateful for, including having her own life to live. She no longer had to fear about anyone telling her what to do or who she had to marry. Jenny was finally free to pursue her own life. And as she looked across the space between her and Mathew, looking up into his face, she wondered how much of her future would be filled with memories of him.

"What are you thinking about?" Mathew asked with a smile on his lips. His question caused Jenny to instantly blush as she looked away from him.

"I was just thinking about all the things that I have to be grateful about," Jenny said. "I'm happy to be back at the ranch, even though the Indians were very nice to me and Mother."

"Are you saying you're enjoying staying here with me?" Mathew asked as his smile grew wider. He was returning the earlier flirting that Jenny had showed him, wondering how far he could go with her.

"Yes, Mathew," Jenny said with a chuckle. "I enjoy staying at the ranch with you… and Bailey." The two laughed as the collie came over to Jenny and settled down at her feet.

"I see how you are. Only here for my dog," Mathew countered as he crossed his arms over his chest in mockery of hurt feelings.

"Yes, Mathew. As soon as I learned you had a cattle dog, I just knew that I had to venture West for Bailey," Jenny retorted as she joined in with his laughter. It felt good to laugh with Mathew, and she realized that the pain in her shoulder had dulled. It was good to be able to laugh freely without worrying about causing pain in her body.

Jenny was surprised when Mathew stood up and began to move his chair. He came to settle next to her and then took her hand in his. She was surprised by the physical touch but found it very pleasant.

"I hope you don't mind, Jenny. I thought it would be nice to simply hold hands," Mathew said as he looked deeply into her eyes. As she saw the kindness in his eyes, she knew that she wanted to do more than just hold his hand.

Leaning forward, Jenny pressed her lips to his. She'd never done anything like this before, never dreamed of being so forward and kissing a man. But she reasoned that since they were courting that a simple kiss would do no harm. But as Mathew raised his free hand and placed it gently to her face, encouraging her, she quickly deepened the kiss as she enjoyed the warmth of his lips on hers.

Mathew broke their kiss as he felt his ardor rising. He found Jenny's gentle kiss to be both alluring, and also very passionate for such a gentle kiss. It was unlike any kiss he'd ever experienced with a woman before and it ignited a burning passion deep inside of him. He had to take several deep breaths to settle his nerves as he continued to stroke his thumb over her cheek.

"What did I do to deserve such a wonderful kiss?" Mathew asked as he finally let his hand fall. But he still held her other hand gently in his. He leaned back in his chair as he watched her with much appreciation.

"You have been so kind and wonderful to me and my mother,"

Jenny said. "You really took a chance on us, on me, and I appreciate that so much." Jenny felt like she was rambling as the excitement of her first kiss ran through her. It had been a thrilling experience, one that she hoped she'd be able go through again with him real soon.

"I'm just glad that everything seems to be working out for you and Margret," Mathew said. He rubbed his thumb over her knuckles as he looked down at her fingers in his. "When I first received your letter, I wasn't quite sure what to think. But I knew that I couldn't just ignore your letter. I wanted to help out anyway I could."

"I'm just lucky that I wrote to you first," Jenny said with a giggle. "I can't imagine what would have happened if I hadn't reached out to you. I simply can't."

"Well, you never have to worry or imagine any longer," Mathew said as he looked back up into her eyes. "You are free to do as you please here, even if I do become worried from time to time."

Jenny chuckled then, enjoying the warmth from her hand in his. "At least you are an honest man, Mathew," she said.

"And I always will be," Mathew vowed. Together they enjoyed a few minutes together, simply being beside one another as their affection for the other continued to grow. But after a time, Jenny knew she would need to get some rest. And so would Mathew since he always rose early to tend to the cattle.

"Well then, let us retire for the night," Jenny said as she withdrew her hand from Mathew's and pushed herself back onto her feet. "The morning waits for no man."

"Wise words from a wise woman," Mathew said as he stood and put his chair back on the other side of the fireplace. He then returned to Jenny and leaned down as he placed a small kiss on her cheek before creating distance between them. "Good night, Jenny."

"Good night, Mathew," Jenny said, wishing he'd kiss her fully on the lips. But knowing she needed rest, she reasoned that it would be best to wait till another time to enjoy the feeling of his lips on hers again. She waited till he was in his room before she made her own way to hers with the candle from the kitchen.

After closing the bedroom door behind her, Jenny set her candle upon the dresser and began to get ready for bed. She had enjoyed bathing earlier in the nice hot water and now felt like she could sleep for days. Dinner had been amazing, she felt alive with emotions as she thought of kissing Mathew. She could tell that they had a deep connection and were obviously attracted to one another. Now, as she blew out the candle and got back into bed, she wondered how long it would take Mathew to propose to her.

# CHAPTER 17

The following days seemed to bring everyone at the ranch a peaceful routine and evenings to look forward to. Jenny felt she was growing stronger each day as the pain in her shoulder slowly faded away. But each passing day brought the coldness of winter. And as November 1st came to Bear Creek, so did the first snow of the year.

Never having seen such fluffy snow before, Jenny stood on the front porch one morning, her cloak wrapped around her as she watched the white snow fall from the sky. She was mesmerized by it and reached out her hand to feel a snowflake fall on her skin. It was the largest snowflake she'd ever seen and she watched as the landscape quickly turned to pure white. After a while, Margret joined her daughter on the porch, passing her a tin cup of coffee to keep her warm. She too thought the snow was very lovely but was worried about keeping warm as they traveled to and from town. Right now, the snow seemed very tame, but if the wind picked up, it would be brutal to make the trip.

"What do you want to do today?" Margret asked Jenny as they sipped their coffee and looked out over the snow-covered landscape.

They thankfully didn't have to be in town that day for housekeeping and could remain safe at home.

"How about we do some baking? Then when the snow stops we can take the wagon into town to give Mrs. Tibet some fresh baked cookies or perhaps a pie?" Jenny suggested.

"If we are going to bake today, we should also make something for Brown Bear and his people. I'm thinking sugar cookies because they look easy to make and you can make a lot of them in a short time," Margret replied.

"That sounds delicious," Jenny said as she headed back inside with her mother. Though she loved watching the fluffy snow fall, she also liked how warm the ranch house stayed. Mathew had taken the time to replenish their stack of wood by the fireplace yesterday and today Jenny didn't have to worry about going outside to get more wood.

"How about we add a bit of nutmeg and cinnamon? Wouldn't that be festive?" Margret said as the idea came to mind.

"Someone's becoming a bit adventurous with her cooking," Jenny teased as they hung up their cloaks before pulling on their aprons. They set their tins in the sink before gathering supplies from the pantry.

"Sometimes I believe the best way to cook is to make food based on what you are feeling," Margret explained. "This snow reminds me of the holidays, and I think it would be nice to make holiday cookies."

"I agree, Mother."

After reviewing the recipe, they started mixing together the ingredients for the sugar cookies. They were so lost in chatter that they didn't even hear when someone knocked on the front door. It was only when the sound came again, and much louder, that they halted what they were doing.

"Mathew wouldn't knock," Jenny said as she wiped her hands on her apron. She wasn't sure who was visiting them and was worried about strangers.

"Well, let's go see who it is. It's cold outside today, anyways." Together, the women went to the door, and after taking a deep breath,

Jenny pulled it open. They were both surprised as they watched Brown Bear step into the ranch house followed by a few of his braves.

"Brown Bear, what an unexpected surprise." Jenny smiled at the man as she shut the door. The Indians were dressed in long buckskin trousers and tunics and wore buffalo furs around their shoulders.

"The best of surprises are often unexpected," Brown Bear said as he knocked off the snow that had collected on his shoulders. He and a few of his tribe had ridden through the forest to visit with their friends. He knew that it would be too difficult for Jenny to travel with the wagon through the forest, and Mathew always had Daniel with him in the pasture.

"Well, please come in and have a seat at the table," Margret said as she gestured to the dining table. Brown Bear relayed the offer to his braves, and soon they settled down. "Would you like some coffee?" Brown Bear didn't particularly like the dark black liquid, but he also did not want to be rude to his hosts.

"We will take just a bit." He told his braves that the women were preparing them coffee, and Brown Bear couldn't help but laugh when they grimaced. Thankfully, the women had already gone to the kitchen to prepare the drink, and they returned shortly with several tin cups of coffee and a plate of cookies.

"We were making these to bring to the Indian camp when the snow settled," Jenny explained. Brown Bear looked at the plate of cookies, experimentally picked one up and tried just a bit. He was surprised by its sweetness and quickly finished it before taking another.

"I do not think the snow will stop till next season," Brown Bear said once he'd had his fill. He liked the cookie very much and hoped that Jenny and Margret would make more soon. "That is why I came. To tell you to be prepared for this winter. I predict lots of snow." Jenny and Margret looked at one another then.

"That is what we are most worried about," Margret said. "It will be hard to travel with the snow on the ground." Brown Bear grunted as he nodded in agreement.

"That is why we have brought you an Indian pony," Brown Bear declared. "It will bear you both and will be able to travel in the snow." Jenny was shocked to hear this and glanced at her mother to see that she had the same expression on her face.

"We have never ridden Indian ponies before," Margret said, thinking she barely knew how to ride a regular horse.

Brown Bear chuckled. "Most White women have not." The Indian braves laughed with Brown Bear once he explained the joke. "Come. We shall teach you how to ride Indian pony." The Indian Chief and his braves rose from the table so quickly, it was hard to follow after them. But Jenny and Margret gathered their bonnets and cloaks and bundled up for the cold weather as they stepped outside with the Indians.

Several Indian ponies stood out front of the ranch house, barely tethered to the hitching post by a rope around their necks. Just as Brown Bear had stated, the amount of snow on the ground was much more than what Jenny and Margret had seen earlier. Taking a pony from the hitching post, Brown Bear led it away from the house and then motioned for Jenny and Margret to come close.

"This pony should be good for you two," Brown Bear explained. "I shall show you how to mount it." Jenny realized that the pony had no saddle and that it would be necessary for them to ride bareback. And when Brown Bear threw his weight over the horse in a graceful leap, both Jenny and Margret were certain they'd never be able to do something like that in their lives. Seeing their shocked expressions, the Indian braves did laugh at them. But when Margret gave them a stern look, they quickly quieted once more.

"This is going to take some practice, Brown Bear," Jenny said, looking up at the Indian upon the pony.

"It is a good thing we've already had our coffee then," Brown Bear said as he laughed. He then hopped down from the pony as though it was no difficult task. For an older man, he was certainly light on his feet.

For the next hour or so, Jenny and Margret practiced lifting themselves on and off the pony. At one point Jenny felt bad for the pony, but watching the horse closely, it did not seem to mind. And though there came a time when Jenny felt comfortable with running a short distance and swinging herself up onto the pony, her mother had made little progress.

"Here, let us try this," Brown Bear said as he led the pony over to the front porch. "Margret, try from the top step here." Brown Bear pointed at it, and Margret figured a boost would do her good. Now a bit higher off the ground, Margret was able to make her way onto the pony behind Jenny with little effort.

Jenny folded her fingers into the pony's mane as Margret wrapped her arms around her. She was nervous about being upon the pony and hoped that Jenny would figure out how to lead it without using reins. Snow continued to fall, but the pony seemed to be unaffected by the rising snow line as Brown Bear led it around the front of the ranch house while showing Jenny how to instruct it to do what she wanted.

"The pony will sense what you need before you tell it," Brown Bear explained. "Become one with the pony and it will never fail you."

"You make learning to ride very poetic," Jenny commented as she learned to lead the pony around a short distance.

"What does this word mean, 'poetic'?" Brown Bear asked as he looked up at the young woman on the pony.

"It means that your words sound beautiful as you describe how to ride an Indian pony," Jenny explained. Brown Bear simply shrugged his shoulders in response, small mounds of snow that had gathered once again on his shoulders fell to the ground. After practicing for a bit longer, Jenny and Margret then hopped off the pony and led it inside the barn to be settled into a stall.

"Indian ponies are not used to being in a house," Brown Bear explained. "You must let the pony out of this house every morning and only let it back in when it becomes very cold outside."

"We promise to take good care of the pony." Margret wasn't thrilled over the idea of riding the pony in and out of town and wondered what her new friends would think about her mounted on an Indian pony. But since the weather was only getting colder and it was bound to snow more in Montana than Virginia, Margret told herself it was important that she be thankful for the pony so she could still make it to town to visit with her new friends.

"Very good," Brown Bear said. He then nodded to his Indian braves as they returned to their own ponies.

"Wait!" Jenny said as she rushed towards the ranch house. "Don't forget your cookies." Brown Bear nodded, a smile coming to his face as Jenny ducked into the house and quickly returned with a small basket.

"Thank you, Jenny. I shall share these, but hope you'll make more soon for me," Brown Bear said as he laughed.

"Certainly, Brown Bear." Together with her mother, Jenny stood on the front porch as the snow continued to fall. They waved as the Indians left the ranch, disappearing into the trees.

"My goodness, who would have thought that Indians would visit us today," Margret said as she led Jenny back into the house. 'And bring us a pony!'

"Certainly not I," Jenny replied as they laughed together over learning to ride an Indian pony. After putting away their bonnets and cloaks, and after Jenny put more logs on the fire, they returned to baking more cookies.

# CHAPTER 18

That morning when the snow had started to fall, Mathew thought it was a magical sight to see. The first snow of the year always seemed to be such a beautiful sight, but as it continued to fall throughout the day, he was quickly reminded of how much he didn't like the snow. He slowly grew colder and colder, having to hop down from Daniel and walk around just to warm up. He urged the cattle to stay active and warm as well, but as the day grew longer, the more he looked forward to returning to the warmth of the ranch house.

When Mathew finally decided to head in, Bailey bounding through the snow as though it didn't bother the collie in the least, he was surprised to see an Indian pony in the barn. The pony neighed at Mathew as he came in and seemed to talk to Daniel as Mathew settled the horse in for the night. Mathew was certainly curious to know how it came to be in his barn and quickly made his way into the house the moment the horses were all fed and ready for a cold night.

The house smelled of cinnamon and the holidays as Mathew entered. He inhaled deeply, enjoying the pleasant aromas. Jenny was setting the table as he entered, and as their eyes locked, they smiled brightly at one another. Mathew instantly remembered the kiss they'd shared not that long ago and looked forward to having a similar experience soon.

"I see we have a new addition to the ranch," Mathew said as he gestured behind him towards the barn. Bailey barked happily and ran a few times around the dining table before settling on the rug in front of the fire.

"You'll never believe it, but Brown Bear came and delivered the pony today with a few of his braves," Jenny explained. "He taught me and Mother how to ride it in hopes that we will be able to make it into town when the snow is high." Mathew was stunned to hear this as he took off his coat and boots at the door.

"That was very gracious of him," Mathew said as he came towards Jenny.

"We also made sugar cookies today and made sure to send a few dozen with him back to the camp," Margret added as she came and set down a hot loaf of bread on the table. It had risen nicely and was golden brown on all sides.

"That looks like an amazing loaf of bread," Mathew said.

"Thank you," Margret said proudly before returning to the kitchen.

"So, Brown Bear said he wanted you two to have the pony for work?" Mathew said as he rubbed his hands together. They were still very cold. But he was curious about Brown Bear's motives.

"Yes, that's what he said," Jenny confirmed. "Why? What do you think?" Mathew thought about it for a second before a smile came to his face.

"I think Brown Bear also wanted to give you a way to come visit him at the Indian camp," Mathew said. "Perhaps the maidens miss having your company." Jenny laughed at the thought.

"Brown Bear is a very clever man," Jenny said. Mathew nodded as he went over to the fire to warm himself.

"He has always been since I've known him," Mathew agreed. Jenny and Margret finished setting the table then, and once Mathew felt warm once more, he sat down at the table with Bailey at his feet.

"Tomorrow we plan to take cookies to Mrs. Tibet," Margret said. "We have Frys to tidy up and will make sure to leave some for them as well."

"The house certainly smells amazing so I'm sure the cookies are as well," Mathew said between bites of roast. Margret had prepared a beef roast that they'd purchased from the butcher on their way back from town the other day. The cold weather had helped to preserve the meat, and it had tasted wonderful once completed in the oven with potatoes and carrots. Jenny had spent the afternoon cleaning up after their cookie experiments and doing her best to tidy around the house.

After dinner, Mathew was able to confirm that the cookies were indeed delicious, and after cleaning up after dinner, Margret said goodnight to give the young couple time alone. Jenny always looked forward to this time with Mathew and was thankful that her mother was so considerate.

"So, what do you think of riding an Indian pony?" Mathew asked as they settled down beside the fire together.

"I think it's harder to ride than a horse because there is no saddle or reins to control the pony with," Jenny explained. "It's like the pony senses where you want to go and how fast you want to travel and just does it while you hang on." Mathew chuckled as he nodded in understanding. He'd ridden an Indian pony once and found it to be very different from his Daniel.

"I hope it will be useful to you and Margret," Mathew said. "It is only going to be getting colder, and I'm afraid you won't be able to make it into town very often even with the Indian pony." Jenny nodded, having had the same thought earlier.

"I know that it's too cold sometimes to travel outside," Jenny reasoned. "But Mother and I need to keep up our jobs if we are going to continue affording the things we need. We only have so much money in the bank." Mathew also knew how much the women enjoyed going to town and getting to visit with everyone. He was certain that the older couples enjoyed their company as well.

"If you don't mind me asking, how much do you and your mother have saved up?" Mathew asked. He hoped he could be of some assistance if he was more familiar with their financial situation.

"About fifteen thousand dollars," Jenny said with a sigh. "And to think that is a small sum compared to what Mother used to have." Mathew's eyes had gone wide at hearing the amount. He had to tell himself over and over what she'd just said if he was going to hear her correctly.

"What's the matter, Mathew?" Jenny asked once she saw the strange look on his face.

"Jenny, my dear, do you realize how wealthy that makes you out here?" Mathew asked. With that type of money, he didn't even understand why the women had been working at all. With that fortune he could not only double his herd but hire cattle hands to tend to the herd for him.

"I suppose I do not," Jenny said, feeling a bit embarrassed. "It is such a small amount compared to what I was born into. Mother and I did sell many of our fine pieces of jewelry before making our way out West." Mathew did his best to regain his composure, not wanting Jenny to feel uncomfortable. He couldn't imagine how fifteen thousand dollars was a small amount and what her family's fortune used to be to consider that amount small.

"Jenny, that amount of money means you and your mother wouldn't need to work for a long time," Mathew started with. "If I had that much money, I would buy more cattle and start hiring cattle hands to help me with the work."

Jenny looked at Mathew as he spoke, trying to see his point of view. The idea of not working didn't settle well with Jenny. She was very proud of her accomplishments and was finding joy in her work. She also felt good to know that she was helping others out.

"Well, Mother and I like our work so much that I don't think we'd quit," Jenny said. "And I'd be willing to help you with the herd as a type of business investment." If their savings could help Mathew, then she'd always be willing to help the person that had helped her family so much in the past few months.

Mathew ran his fingers through his long brown hair, trying to think of his words carefully. He didn't want Jenny to feel obligated to help him out. It was certainly not his intention at all. Taking a moment to gather his thoughts, he stood up and moved his chair to Jenny's side before settling down next to her. Jenny giggled as she shook her head at him.

"You should just leave your chair there so we can sit next to each other every evening," she said.

"You know, I like that idea a lot," Mathew said as he leaned towards her, looking deeply into her eyes. "Jenny, I like the thought of spending every evening together with you and hope you'll seriously consider becoming my wife." Jenny was so surprised by his words that she didn't say anything right away. She just stared into his eyes, wondering if all of this was some sort of dream.

"Are you asking me to marry you, Mathew?" Jenny asked, not quite sure what he had meant.

"Yes, Jenny," Mathew said. "I want to marry you. And not just because you're wealthy. But because I like the idea of spending every day with you." Jenny thought about his words, feeling the truth in them.

"Mathew, I'd be happy to marry you," Jenny said as a bright smile came to her face. "I want to marry you because I love you." It was Mathew's turn now to be shocked as her words of affection washed over him.

"You really love me?" Mathew asked as a grand smile came across his face. Jenny nodded smiling her warm smile. "Oh, Jenny. I love you, too."

As soon as the words were out, Mathew bent and pressed his lips to Jenny's. Warmth spread through their bodies from the impact of the kiss. Mathew placed both hands on either side of Jenny's face as he held her close to him and kissed her soundly. Jenny closed her eyes and let Mathew lead the way, passion blooming between them as a cord of love was wrapped around them. Never before had she felt anything like this for anyone, and to think that she'd fallen in love with a cowboy from Montana thrilled her.

Mathew slowly brought the kiss to an end as he lowered his hands from Jenny's face, letting them settle in hers. He looked deeply into her eyes, never before thinking that he'd ever feel this way for a woman. He was truly in love with Jenny and looked forward to the day when they could get married and forever seal their fate together.

"I think I could get used to that," Jenny said shyly as she gazed into Mathew's hazel eyes.

"Have you ever kissed a man before?" Mathew asked, realizing that not everyone was as experienced as he was when it came to passion.

Jenny shook her head as a deep blush settled on her face. "You are the first man I've ever kissed," she confessed. Mathew swallowed hard as he thought of his next question, feeling like he already knew the answer.

"Does that also mean you've never been with a man before, in bed?" Mathew asked carefully. Jenny could not help but giggle as she shook her head.

"I've been saving myself for marriage," Jenny explained. Mathew nodded, knowing that it was very genuine of Jenny. She'd never come across as someone who would mislead someone into her bed.

"I'm very honored then to not only be your first kiss, but to one day soon becoming your first in every way," Mathew said as he reached into his pocket and pulled out his mother's ring. He'd been carrying it in his pocket ever since Jenny had agreed to be courted by him. It was a simple gold band with a single diamond in the center. Probably nothing as fancy as Jenny might have been used to in Virginia, but as he slipped it onto her finger, she looked down at it with sparkling eyes and a bright smile.

"It's gorgeous, Mathew," Jenny said as she held her hand out to see better in the glow of the fire.

"It was my mother's," Mathew explained. "My father gave it to me so that one day I too may be happily married."

"Oh, Mathew. I shall cherish it forever," Jenny exclaimed before she wrapped her arms around Mathew and rested her head on his shoulder. She was so overjoyed that she could hardly contain herself. And feeling Mathew near her seemed to fill her with even more excitement. "I can't wait to tell Mother in the morning."

Mathew chuckled as he wrapped his arms around Jenny. "Then we should probably get some sleep so morning comes," Mathew suggested. Jenny leaned back and looked up into his eyes, hardly believing that she would one day soon be married.

"Only if you insist," she teased as she let her hands fall from Mathew before pushing herself up from the chair.

"Oh, I dearly insist, my dear," Mathew said with a sly smile. "Till tomorrow, then." He leaned down and planted a kiss on her forehead before whistling for Bailey to follow him to their room. As Jenny watched Mathew disappear into his room, she knew that one day she'd also follow Mathew to their bedroom and experience what marriage was all about. The thought filled her with excitement that as she went to her own room, she wondered if she'd ever be able to get any sleep.

As Jenny lay in bed, she looked at the ring on her finger in the moonlight. She could hardly believe the day had come that she was officially taken by someone. If they'd been in Virginia, the announcement would have been run in the paper in the morning and a large engagement party would have been planned. But as Jenny lay in bed and thought about all of that fuss, she knew that simply telling her mother in the morning and sharing the news with their new friends in town would be satisfying enough for her. She smiled to herself as she drifted off to sleep, the covers tucked under her chin.

# CHAPTER 19

The news of Jenny and Mathew's engagement ran through the town like wildfire. Jenny and Margret had made it into town on the Indian pony, and Jenny couldn't help but show Mr. and Mrs. Fry her ring. And since the older couple that owned the dry goods store knew everyone, it wasn't long before everyone knew the big news.

"Oh, there is going to be a wedding in Bear Creek!" Mr. Fry exclaimed once Jenny had shared her story.

"And you must let me make your dress," Mrs. Fry quickly added.

"That is very kind of you, Mrs. Fry," Margret had said, surprised by the woman's offer. She and Jenny had talked about ordering something from a catalogue, but was worried about it arriving with all the snow on the ground.

"It would be my pleasure," Mrs. Fry said with a beaming smile. "It's not every day that a young woman gets married in Bear Creek." And so as the news spread, so did the plans for the wedding. As soon as Pastor Barthelme Munster was expected back in town, the wedding would take place. Jenny and Margret felt like there was plenty to organize, but the town's people seemed eager to help as well.

In the evenings, Margret and Jenny would talk with Mathew about their time in town, the people's response to their wedding, and how many people were willing to help out. "Mr. and Mrs. Tibet even said that we could have the reception at the inn and that Mrs. Tibet would be willing to cook some food as well," Jenny said with much enthusiasm. Mathew chuckled, loving the way Jenny talked so excitedly. He was pleased to see her so happy about the wedding and looked forward to it himself.

"And of course I offered to help cook," Margret added. "Mathew, what do you think of inviting Brown Bear and his people to the wedding?"

Mathew thought about it for a moment before he nodded. "I think that would be a great idea. I'm sure Brown Bear would feel very honored to be invited," he said.

"Then tomorrow when we go to visit, we shall not only bring cookies but an invitation to the wedding," Jenny suggested. They laughed about it since Brown Bear had become very fond of the women's cookies and looked forward to them every time they went to visit.

"Jenny, would you come with me in the morning before you head to camp?" Mathew asked over dinner one night. "I want to show you the ranch so you understand how large my land is here." Jenny had never thought of it before, and though she saw cattle in the pastures every day, she'd never taken the time to go out and ride around.

"I would love to," Jenny replied.

It was early morning when Jenny and Mathew stepped out onto the front porch of the ranch house. The sun was peeking over the horizon, sending hues of pink and blue into the clouds above. It was cold with a fresh layer of snow on the ground, but it was not windy so the cold did not burn their cheeks. Bundled up in layers, Mathew led Jenny to the barn to collect Daniel so he could show Jenny the extent of the property. Margret was already working on a fresh batch of cookies and would be ready by the time they returned.

Once the draft horse had been saddled with a few blankets below the saddle to keep him warm, Jenny pulled herself up into the saddle first.

"You're really getting good at that," Mathew said as he did the same, coming to sit behind her on the saddle.

"I had a good teacher," Jenny said over her shoulder as she looked at her husband-to-be. Seeing Mathew every morning and evening filled Jenny with so much joy that she really looked forward to any time they got to spend alone together. And as Mathew led the horse out of the barn and into the pasture, she relished the feeling of him being so close to her.

Mathew sent Daniel into a fast trot as they made their way through the pasture. Cattle scattered out of their path as Bailey barked happily at them to get them to move. The collie zipped all over the pasture with such speed that Jenny couldn't help but laugh at the sight.

"I didn't know he could run so fast," Jenny admitted.

"That's because Bailey is no doubt showing off for you," Mathew replied. Mathew led the horse further into the pasture, the herd staying close to the barn and their food source. He'd have to drive the herd later to keep them warm and strong. But for now, he was simply enjoying being with Jenny.

"This pasture ends here at this gate and the next one begins over there," Mathew said as he pointed to where one ended and the other began "In the warm seasons, I move the herd from one pasture to the other so they can eat the grass and stay healthy."

"It seems to go on forever," Jenny exclaimed as she looked far into the distance to try to see the end of the other pasture. "It must take a lot of hard work to maintain it all."

"It certainly does," Mathew agreed with a sigh. "I own over 50 acres of property with the potential of fencing off most pastures. It just can be a hassle to be checking on the fences every week to make sure there are not any broken-down boards. One day, I hope to increase the size of the herd as more cows give birth. Maybe even hire a ranch hand or two to keep up with the maintenance of the ranch."

"Don't worry, Mathew. You don't have to do this on your own anymore. I'll be here to help," Jenny said with much conviction in her voice. Mathew chuckled as he wrapped his free arm around her and held her close to him.

"Are you going to start coming out here with me to tend to the pasture and cattle?" Mathew asked.

"My goodness, no," Jenny said with a snort. "But with Mother and me working, and with our combined money in the bank, I'm sure we could hire someone to come out here and help you in return." Mathew thought about it for a few minutes as they looked over the expanse of his land. He didn't know how he felt about using some of Jenny's money to fund his dream but knew that it was better to think about the matter than just say no right away.

"For now, my dear, let us simply focus on the wedding," Mathew said as he turned Daniel around and headed back towards the ranch house. Jenny always enjoyed thinking about the wedding and couldn't wait to finally be Mathew's wife.

At the front of the ranch house, Mathew and Jenny parted ways. Jenny went inside to help her mother finish baking the cookies and getting them ready to travel. And once they were ready, Jenny lead the Indian pony to the front porch where she and Margret got on and headed through the forest to visit with Brown Bear. And just as expected, not only did the Indian Chief and all the children love the cookies, but they also agreed to attend the wedding and to bring traditional celebration dishes to be shared at the reception. For Jenny, it was like a dream come true.

# EPILOGUE

Jenny did her best to take several deep breaths as she stood in the foyer of the church. Just on the other side of the double doors she could hear the eager chatter of all the guests that had come to see her and Mathew wed. Practically all the people in town had come out for the occasion, even though a light snow currently fell outside. She stood next to her mother, and as she turned to look at the older woman, she realized that her mother had been watching her the whole time.

"I don't know why I feel so nervous," Jenny admitted. "It's not like I haven't been in front of a large gathering before."

Margret smiled sweetly at her daughter. She tucked a piece of her auburn hair behind her ear, even though her hair was already perfect. She'd braided it the night before so that this morning it would hang down in ringlets like running water.

"It's normal to be nervous on your wedding day," Margret assured her. "I was nervous when I married your father, even though I knew that we loved each other dearly."

"And I know that Mathew and I are in love," Jenny said. "I just don't know why I feel so jittery." Margret squeezed her shoulder as she chuckled. She realized that no words were going to settle Jenny so instead she looked over her gown. Mrs. Fry had done a splendid job at making a flowing white wedding gown with several layers of detailed lace. Margret would have never found such a lovely gown in any catalogue for Jenny, and she had paid Mrs. Fry handsomely for the custom gown, much to the older woman's surprise and delight.

"You look so beautiful today," Margret said as she fiddled with her veil that had been pinned to the top of Jenny's head and flowed down her back. "I just wish your father was here to see you." Jenny smiled at her mother as she did her best to keep the tears at bay. She'd thought of the same thing that morning as they had prepared to come into town. Mathew had stayed at the inn last night so that Margret and Jenny could have the morning together to get ready and simply spend alone time together.

"I'm sure he is here in spirit, as Brown Bear would say," Jenny reassured her mother. Margret nodded as she quickly wiped the tears from her eyes.

"I believe you are right," Margret said. Then she gasped when she heard the *Wedding March* being played on the organ inside. "It's time," she said excitedly.

Jenny turned her eyes to the chapel as her mother slipped her arm around hers to lead her down the aisle. Once the doors were opened, Jenny didn't bother looking at the crowd that had gathered. She only kept her eyes forward as she searched for Mathew. And as she stepped forward with her mother as the church was filled with beautiful music, her eyes locked with Mathew's.

All the air in Mathew's chest seemed to seep out of him as he saw Jenny being walked down the aisle by her mother. She was a vision of beauty, and Mathew couldn't believe that he was about to marry this angel. Her hair flowed down her shoulders like ribbons of fire. The wedding dress suited her perfectly, was elegant and moved beautifully with her body. He felt like the happiest man in the world as Jenny came to stand in front of him.

"You take good care of her, you hear," Margret said, pulling Mathew's attention away from Jenny for a moment as he held her hands in his. The stern expression on her face startled Mathew for a moment. He swallowed and nodded, and only then did her features relax. Margret than made her way to the front pew next to Brown Bear. Having no family of his own, Mathew had invited his best friends to sit at the front of the church. Next to Brown Bear sat Jacob and Tanner as well.

Time seemed to stop for Mathew and Jenny as Pastor Munster conducted the wedding ceremony. The couple wasn't concerned about the other people in the chapel or really what the pastor was saying. All they could do was look into each other's eyes and feel a sense of peace and immense love for one another. When it came time to repeat their vows, they spoke slowly and clearly, saying each word with conviction, honesty, and promises for a bright future together. And when the ceremony came to an end and the pastor announced them officially married, Mathew kissed Jenny in a way that was a little more passionate than perhaps was appropriate for church. The crowd chuckled in response and a few of them even whistled as Mathew kissed Jenny soundly.

With everything in town being close, it was easy for Mathew and Jenny to lead the wedding procession from the church to the dining room at the inn. Mrs. Tibet and Margret got to work serving dishes on a banquet table, and the Indian maidens added their clay pots of venison stew and blood soup to the spread of food. Jenny enjoyed telling her mother that the blood soup was actually very good, and probably surprised a number of their guests when she enjoyed the soup herself.

There were many people in attendance as they all ate together. Christmas was right around the corner, and it seemed that today's celebration only added to everyone's holiday spirit. Jenny felt like she'd never smiled so much in her life as she visited with everyone and received many special gifts. It was amazing how thoughtful and genuine everyone was. Mathew and she hadn't been gifted any random trinket, but something that would be used and loved for years to come.

Mathew knew that the moment had finally come when he could say his life had been filled. He had a wonderful wife who was independent, feisty, and the best part, loved him dearly. He loved her just as much and looked forward to spending every day with her. And having Margret become part of his family also added to his joy. It was like gaining a second mother, something that he'd dearly missed in his life. And even though the days would grow shorter, colder, and with promises of more snow, none of it bothered him as long as he could have Jenny by his side.

One of the best parts of the whole wedding was getting to see Brown Bear's reaction to it all. It was the first time that the Indians had attended a White person's wedding, and though they had attended in their celebratory garments and received many strange glances from the townspeople, that didn't deter them from enjoying their time in town. Mathew laughed as Brown Bear tried the many different dishes, his plate ending up with cookies and pie.

"Brown Bear, you are going to upset your stomach with that much sugar," Mathew had warned his friend.

"I am always willing to accept a good challenge," Brown Bear had replied as he sat down at their table and began to fill his belly with all the sweet treats. Mathew and Jenny had laughed at the sight and hoped their good friend wouldn't regret his choice later.

At one point in the reception, the chairs and tables had been pushed back against the wall to allow for music and dancing. It had been so long since Jenny had the opportunity to dance that she found it to be a nice surprise. Someone had brought a fiddle to the wedding, and Jenny smiled happily as she saw the town's sheriff begin to play a tune on the string instrument. She was even further surprised to learn that Mathew wasn't a bad dance partner at all.

As they danced around the empty space, the Indians raised their voices in song to a similar tune to the one that Jacob was playing. It shocked everyone, but Jacob didn't dare stop playing. The song was a joyous one, and it filled the room with feelings of happiness and warmth. Jacob finished the song and started into another one, and the Indians simply followed along. Many couples joined Mathew and Jenny in a slow dance, and a few maidens danced in celebration as well.

Jenny never imagined that one day she'd move away from her hometown of Richmond, Virginia. She would have laughed if someone tried to tell her that one day she'd marry a cowboy who lived in Montana. Jenny couldn't believe that she'd not only married the man of her dreams, but also enjoyed the singing and dancing of Indians at their wedding reception. It was certainly a dream come true for Jenny, and a part of her never wanted this reception to end.

During one of the times she and Mathew were resting after another twirl around the dance floor, they were approached by a man and a woman they'd never met before. And since they were both familiar with everyone in town, they were apprehensive about these strangers.

"Congratulations on your wedding," the man said in greeting. He was a tall fellow with black hair and deep green eyes. His body was slim, but his arms looked very muscled as though he was used to hard labor. The woman next to him looked like she could be his twin sister. Jenny recognized the quality of their clothes and figured them to be city people.

"Thank you," Mathew replied. "I'm afraid we are not acquainted."

"Of course, where are my manners," the man said with a chuckle. "My name is Edward James, and this is my sister, Phoebe. We've just bought up the gold mine in the hills right outside of town." Jenny and Mathew stared at the siblings in surprise.

"I can't understand why anyone would want to buy those mines," Mathew replied. "With all due respect, they haven't really been successful." Edward smiled at them as he exchanged a glance with his sister.

"I understand your concern, Mr. Jenkins. Especially after what happened to the last foreman," Edward said honestly. "But we've received some information on where the mines could be expanded to find real gold." There was a twinkling of excitement in Edward's eyes that made Mathew very curious about the man.

"I just ask that you cooperate with the Indian people who also live in the hills, Mr. James," Jenny spoke up. "The Sioux Indians are our friends, as you can see, and we'd hate to see any more trouble between them and the miners."

"Fear not, Mrs. Jenkins," Edward said. "I'm half Indian myself and will make a point to talk to their chief to let him know that I plan to have miners working in the hills as soon as the snow begins to melt." Jenny and Mathew were further surprised by this news. As Jenny studied Edward closely, she could see his darker skin tone that usually came from working out in the sun. She had assumed that it was from such work, but now could see the faint signs of Indian heritage.

"In that case, would you like me to introduce you to Chief Brown Bear?" Mathew offered as he rose from his chair.

"I'd gladly appreciate it," Edward said with a kindly smile. As the gentlemen strolled away, Jenny motioned to the chair next to her for Phoebe to take a seat.

"Thank you, kindly," Phoebe said as she sat down. As Jenny observed her, she didn't see the same Indian heritage in her. She was very curious about the woman.

"My mother and I are originally from Richmond, Virginia," Jenny said, seeing that Phoebe wore a dress similar to the latest fashions when she'd ran away from Richmond with her mother. Phoebe looked at her with a look of unexpected surprise. Jenny chuckled, enjoying whenever she could surprise someone with her own heritage.

"What is a city girl like you doing in a place like this?" Phoebe asked.

"I could say the same for you," Jenny replied, never wanting to tell the tale of her past.

"Is it that obvious?" Phoebe asked as she smoothed down her skirts. The outer layer was clearly silk, an obvious sign that she wasn't from Montana in general.

"I gave up all my silk gowns before coming out West," Jenny said. "I knew that they would do me no good out here." Phoebe nodded, seeming to have recently realized the same thing.

"I think my wardrobe needs to be updated for this type of weather and environment," Phoebe reasoned.

"Don't worry," Jenny said, hoping to reassure the woman. "Mrs. Fry is a wonderful seamstress. She even designed and made my wedding gown."

"My goodness. But it's so lovely," Phoebe said as she looked down at Jenny's long gown.

"That is what I mean. Bear Creek might be a small town, but there are many talented people here," Jenny explained. Phoebe simply nodded as her eyes sought out her brother in the crowd. She hadn't wanted to follow Edward out West, but after the scandal in Boston, she had very little choice in the matter.

"I'm pleased to hear that coming from another city girl," Phoebe replied, curious to know Jenny's own back story. But as she saw how happy the young bride was, she was at least a bit more confident that she and Edward would be content in Bear Creek.

"My brother has been a miner for some time after he refused to take over my father's business in Boston," Phoebe said. She hoped that by sharing some of her family's past that Jenny would be willing to open up to her. "When he got the opportunity to buy this mine, he took the chance. He's convinced that he knows something the last owner did not."

"I do hope he's right," Jenny said with a sigh. "That mine is what kept this town afloat. If it became successful again, this town could really be saved." Phoebe looked at Jenny, wondering just what type of town she and her brother had moved to.

"Well, for now, we must wait out this winter before the mines can be inspected," Phoebe said with a sigh. "We'll be staying here at the inn till we can arrange our own place to stay."

"You'll love Mr. and Mrs. Tibet. They make good company," Jenny said with a smile. "And you'll see me and my mother in town often.

We housekeep for the inn and a few other businesses." Phoebe was surprised to hear that she was a working woman.

"I would have not thought that a family from Richmond would ever need to work for a living," Phoebe said honestly. Jenny smiled, knowing that Phoebe was fishing for information. She'd spent her whole life amongst elite society to understand their designs.

"We don't need to work, per se. But we enjoy the work nonetheless," Jenny explained. "There is something about using your own hands to create something or help someone else out that really brings purpose to me and my mother's life."

"And your husband is a rancher?" Phoebe then asked. Jenny searched for Mathew in the crowd, seeing him sitting with Brown Bear as he introduced the new mine owner to the Indian Chief. She nodded towards Mathew.

"Yes, he is. And a very successful one at that. We have plans to expand the herd in the spring," Jenny said.

"I guess there are a lot of ranchers in the area," Phoebe said as she looked around the room, wondering how long it would take her to learn about the locals and what occupations they had. It was a force of habit to learn everyone's standing in society and place herself above everyone else. It was the way she'd been raised and unfortunately a large part of her downfall in Boston.

"There are also others who own businesses or work for the town. Bear Creek has a mayor, sheriff, deputy, barber, banker, and all sorts of occupations," Jenny said proudly.

"And it looks like there are a lot of men, too," Phoebe observed. Jenny giggled as she nodded.

"Yes, a lot of single men at that," Jenny added. "I'd be careful if I were you. They're going to see a pretty woman such as yourself and try to claim you as their own." Phoebe knew that Jenny said those words in good humor, but a part of her felt quite put off.

"Well, Mrs. Jenkins. I'll be damned if I ever let a man try to claim me again," Phoebe said with a smirk on her lips. Jenny was surprised by her rough words and watched as the woman then stood and walked over to her brother. She couldn't help but smile to herself, wondering how Phoebe would settle into the area and if the mine would ever be truly successful.

The End

=

THANK you for reading and supporting my book and I hope you enjoyed it.

Please will you do me a favor and leave me a review, so I'll know whether you liked it or not, it would be very much appreciated.

# AMELIA'S OTHER BOOKS

**Montana Westward Brides**
   #0 The Rancher's Fiery Bride
   #1 The Reckless Doctor's Bride
   #2 The Rancher's Unexpected Pregnant Bride
   #3 The Lonesome Cowboy's Abducted Bride
   #4 The Sheriff's Stubborn Secretive Bride

# CAST OF CHARACTERS

- **Mathew Jenkins**
- **Jenny Phillips**
- Douglas and Margret Phillips, Jenny's parents
- Duke Phillips, Jenny's uncle
- Mr. & Mrs. Fry, dry goods owner, seamstress
- Jacob Benning, sheriff
- Tanner Williams, deputy
- Pastor Barthelme Munster, traveling pastor
- Mr. & Mrs. Tibet, inn owners
- Mr. Demetri Franklin, mayor of Bear Creek
- Louis Fritz, bank owner
- Curtis Denver, butcher
- Brown Bear, leader of the Sioux Indian camp
- Dan Mavis, schoolteacher and tutor
- Mitchel Franks, barber
- Dr. Harvey, local doctor

# CONNECT WITH AMELIA

Visit my website at **www.ameliarose.info** to view my other books and to sign up to my mailing list so that you are notified about my new releases and special offers.

# ABOUT AMELIA ROSE

Amelia is a shameless romance addict with no intentions of ever kicking the habit. Growing up she dreamed of entertaining people and taking them on fantastical journeys with her acting abilities, until she came to the realization as a college sophomore that she had none to speak of. Another ten years would pass before she discovered a different means to accomplishing the same dream: writing stories of love and passion for addicts just like herself. Amelia has always loved romance stories and she tries to tie all the elements she likes about them into her writing.